EDGE

A man with memories. Unhappy memories. Bloody memories. Of disease, cruelty and starvation. Of Andersonville prison camp—the most horror-filled in the Civil War.

The man in the next cell would like him to forget.

But Edge is a man alone—with his memories. A man who has waited a long time for vengeance.

WARNING

This story is not for the faint-hearted reader.

THE EDGE SERIES:

EDGE: RED RIVER

by
George G. Gilman

PINNACLE BOOKS • LOS ANGELES

EDGE: RED RIVER

A Pinnacle Book, formerly titled *Edge: The Blue, The Grey and The
Red*, published by special arrangement with New English Library,
Limited.

ISBN 0-523-40536-7

First printing, May 1973
Second printing, May 1975
Third printing, December 1977
Fourth printing, September 1978

Printed in the United States of America

PINNACLE BOOKS, INC.
2029 Century Park East
Los Angeles, California 90067

For
M.P.
who, like Edge, has
Scandinavian connections

AUTHOR'S NOTE

Although this novel is complete in itself, it does continue the Civil War adventures of Edge (then Captain Josiah S. Hedges) which began in *Killer's Breed*.

CHAPTER ONE

There were four men and one woman in the small back room of the Royal Flush saloon at the bay end of Market Street. The game was five-card draw any pair to open and two of the men were cheating. Drew Shelby was the expert, dealing over the top of the shiny lid of a tin tobacco box. Abel Heffner caught his signals and acted upon them. Chadwick Eden lost steadily and didn't care, as he alternately lifted a shot glass to his lips and caressed the well-rounded right hip of Emmeline Greer standing by his side. The fourth man folded automatically on Shelby's deal and played the value of his hand when the cards came from a different source. He won more often than he lost.

The atmosphere within the room was fetid with sweat, cigarette smoke, rye whiskey and the woman's unsubtle perfume: liberally mixed and laced with the oily smell of the kerosene lamp that dropped yellow light on to the worn green baize of the table covering. It was late, with night pressing a warm blackness against the small square window. The game was three hours old and the cards were greasy from oozing pores. Emmeline Greer was bored with it but held her peace because Eden had paid her price for the whole night. The saloon had become quiet a long time previously and from the silence that infiltrated the room from beyond, the entire city of San Francisco could have been dead.

"One more hand," Eden said as he drained the bottle into his glass and Shelby picked up the deck to give them a gambler's shuffle.

He had just lost a big pot to Heffner but this was not the reason for his sudden disenchantment with the game. His hand had sought and found a higher and more resilient area of the woman's body and she had stooped slightly to allow him the privilege. As his hand cupped her large breast, his handsome face, aged beyond its years by an excess of hard liquor, lost the easy half smile with which he had viewed his apparent run of ill luck, and expressed blatant lust. The woman, who was not pretty but had the voluptuousness of body that guaranteed her security of employment, fixed a self-satisfied smirk upon her round face.

"Hell, your luck has got to change," Shelby encouraged. He was about fifty, which made him twice Eden's age, and he spoke to the younger man in a paternal tone. He was a big man, with the height and shoulders of a lumberjack: but his hands were soft and supple. Dealing cards was the hardest work he had done in a long time.

"Yeah," Heffner agreed. "Stay in, young man. The time to stop is when you're ahead."

Heffner looked more like a professional gambler. He was pushing sixty and his hair was already white. He had a kindly face which hinted at a lack of intelligence and a surfeit of good nature. His frame was slight and he had the same kind of hands as his partner.

Emmeline bent her body more firmly into the greasy palm of Eden. The young man looked up at her and his drunken eyes saw the promise and heightened their determination. His fingers stretched, reaching above the neckline of the low-cut dress and began to trace tiny patterns on the soft curve of flesh.

"Maybe you'll get a pat royal this time," Shelby pressed on, showing tobacco-stained teeth in a grin. But his grey eyes continued to be flat and dead.

"He seems to be happy with the pair he's already got," the fourth player said evenly.

He was the tallest man at the table. He reached to six feet three inches and his build was composed of almost two hundred pounds arranged in muscular proportion that implied latent strength without emphasizing it. His handsomeness was of the essentially masculine type to an extent where he was often considered ugly. His features were angular and the burnished skin tone of the toughened, much-lined flesh of his face hinted strongly of Mexican blood in his veins. And it was true that his father came from Sonara. But the Scandinavian heritage of his mother could be seen in the piercing blueness of his narrow, deep-set eyes. At the start of the game he had been freshly bathed and shaved, but the ingrained dirt of the trail was beginning to come to the surface with sweat, and stubble was sprouting, as black as his shoulder-length hair and the moustache that grew along the top of his thin mouth and turned down sharply at each corner. He looked mean and incapable of smiling, even at his own humor. His name was Edge.

Eden laughed. "Hey, I like that."

"I can see you do," Edge said as he watched the young man's fingers dig deeper into the swell of the woman's breast.

Shelby sighed and began to deal. Each card passed over the top of the tin's reflective surface. Eden released his grip on the woman with reluctance and finished his drink at a swallow. Each man gathered up his cards and fanned them. Edge looked at his three tens, king and queen. On the table in front of him

9

was better than twenty-seven hundred dollars, which put him more than two hundred ahead of when he started. The other three, all with bigger bankrolls, regarded their cards with expressions carved from stone.

Eden couldn't open and Edge started the pot with a twenty-dollar bill. The others stayed in. Edge discarded his queen and drew one. It came deftly off the bottom and gave him a full house. Heffner stayed with what he had and Shelby and Eden each drew one. Edge kept the ante at twenty but folded when everybody stayed in the game and Shelby rubbed the left side of his nose with a long index finger. Heffner raised by fifty and the other two went along with him. Edge stacked his money into a neat pile and pushed it into the hip pocket of his worn pants. Then he took out the makings and began to roll a cigarette. He formed a perfect cylinder by touch, for his eyes, glinting like slivers of blue glass, moved across the faces of the other three men as they pushed bills into the centre of the table. There was over one thousand dollars in the pot when Shelby ran his tongue along his top lip and Heffner sighed dramatically and folded his hand.

"I'm out," he said with disappointment, and threw his cards carelessly on the baize.

Shelby allowed himself a small smile with his mouth. "Let's make it interesting," he murmured and counted out five one-hundred-dollar bills. He tossed the money into the pot. "Give you a chance to get some of your money back, son."

Eden was not holding his cards. They were spread out on the table before him. The fingers of one hand were moving on Emmeline's hip again, as he toyed with his money with the other. Although he was either too drunk or too preoccupied to realize he was

10

being set up, he knew how to play poker. His youthful face betrayed no sign of what he was thinking.

"Your five hundred, and a thousand more," he challenged.

Heffner drew in his breath sharply and the sound was magnified by the silence in the room. The match flaring from friction with Edge's boot heel was like a minor explosion. Shelby acted out a few moments of indecision, then picked up two bills.

"Your thousand, and up by a like amount. Makes it expensive to see, don't it?"

"Glad I ain't in it," Heffner said.

Edge lit his cigarette and blew smoke across the table. It was grey, but turned blue as it billowed around the lamp. Eden released the woman and seemed about to pick up his cards. His hands, rich with two decorated rings, hovered, then settled on his money. "I'll pay," he said, and covered Shelby's bet. Then, impatiently, he flipped over his cards to show a straight to the queen.

"It's not your night, son," Shelby said with phony sadness as he spread his hand.

Disappointment showed momentarily in Eden's dark eyes, but was superceded by resignation as the fact of the four aces imprinted itself on his mind. He started to rise, gathering up the remnants of his bankroll as Shelby hauled in the pot.

"It's about time you did some screwing of your own," Edge said softly.

Everybody froze and for a moment it was like a waxworks tableau, with all eyes fastened upon the tall man's expressionless face.

"You implying something, mister?" Shelby demanded darkly.

Edge reached out a brown-skinned hand and turned over Heffner's cards. The man had been betting without even a pair of two spots.

11

"It's a game of bluff," Heffner said, a nervous tremor distorting the words.

"Ain't up to me, kid," Edge said, talking to Eden but locking his stare upon Shelby. "But you've been taken to the cleaners. The price was too high and you're left with egg on your face."

Emmeline looked frightened and tugged at Eden's coat sleeve. "Come on, Chad. Let's go."

He shook free and his eyes moved from Edge to Shelby and back again. Comprehension seemed to be a long time coming.

"You don't want trouble son," Heffner said quickly, and swallowed hard. "Your mother wouldn't like that."

The mention of his mother had a sobering effect on the young man. His eyes were suddenly clear and he shed the years as if somebody had waved a magic wand. He looked like a boy, frustrated and helpless.

"Go and have fun," Shelby said, trying to inject lightness into his tone. But there was a strong sense of purpose in the way he raked the money to him and began to stack it.

"I don't like being taken for a sucker, Shelby," Eden snarled, straightening suddenly, so that his chair toppled over backwards.

The woman sprang away from him with a small cry, as if she had been hurt. Shelby had the fast reactions of a man who lived by his wits. The gun he jerked from a shoulder holster under his jacket was a Continental Arms .22 pepperbox with an ornate grip.

"He ain't heeled!" Heffner yelled, his voice pitched high from fear.

Eden's suddenly pale face was tacit confirmation of the fact and he started to raise his empty hands in a gesture of pathetic surrender. But Shelby's knuckle was already whitening around the trigger and the killer instinct was hot behind his eyes.

12

"He is!" he snarled and turned the six-hole barrel of the tiny gun towards Edge.

Edge snapped the Colt from his tied-down holster and fired across the table. The bullet ploughed a furrow along the baize and kicked up shredded paper as it penetrated Shelby's winnings. Then it drilled a neat hole high in the man's stomach and blood sprayed the table, garishly red in the soft yellow light. Emmeline screamed as Shelby's eyes closed. But the cry was silenced by the explosion of the pepperbox. Shelby began to fall backwards, his gun hand rising as his arm stayed iron stiff. The bullet went high and rang against the burnished metal of the lamp, ricocheting into a spinning trajectory at an acute angle. As Shelby hit the back of his chair and then toppled sideways, Eden screamed and began to crumple. He hit the floor, the scream becoming a whimper, then nothing. Blood was a liquid curtain across one cheek, spreading from the scarlet slash of his eye socket.

Death clamped a tight grip of stillness over the room for long seconds as the gunsmoke retreated into the darkness above the lamp. Then Heffner cursed and leaned sideways to look at his partner.

"You killed Drew!" he said hoarsely, as if he couldn't believe the truth of his own words.

Edge rested the barrel of the Colt on the table, altering the aim slightly so that it was pointed at Heffner. "Him or me?" he posed.

Heffner looked up, saw the gun and nodded vigorously. "Sure, mister. It was self-defence. I saw that."

"Chad's alive!" the woman exclaimed, crouching down beside the young man. "We've got to get a doctor for him."

She straightened up and started to turn towards the door. Without allowing his attention to wander for an instant, Edge slid off his chair and sidestepped around the table to where Eden was curled up, silent and still bleeding badly from the eye. Heffner watched him nervously, starkly aware of the narrowed eyes and aimed revolver. Edge reached for the injured man's hand, fingers searching out a pulse. He found it, weak and slow. But in the next instant he had released the limp wrist and begun to turn, aware that something about the room had altered. Eden's shot glass still stood on the tabletop. There was merely a wet ring to mark the spot where the empty bottle had been.

Emmeline Greer put every ounce of her considerable strength into the downward blow and made the connection just as Edge saw her. The bottle hit him precisely in the center of his head, shattering and scattering tiny shards of glass among his hair. He saw the sadistic satisfaction in her eyes, then felt the burning heat of pain as the darkness descended, turning as red as the blood on Eden's face. He toppled forward as his muscleless legs folded. His fingers loosened their grip on the Colt and the gun skittered across the bare boards of the floor. The death rattle was a dry trickling sound deep within Eden's throat.

"Christ, lady!" Heffner yelled as he leapt to his feet. "Will he hate you."

"It comes higher than loving me," Emmeline muttered as she tossed aside the broken neck of the bottle and stooped to tug the bankroll from Edge's hip pocket.

Heffner took a moment to realize what was happening, then gathered the money from the tabletop, his greedy fingers staying clear of those bills stained by Shelby's blood. The woman was not so squeamish and raked up what was left, pushing all the bills down into her ample cleavage. Voices sounded from above and bootless feet slapped the floor.

"They woke up," Heffner stammered.

"Two here won't," Emmeline snapped in reply as

14

she headed for the rear door, her long dress swishing.

"What about Marshal Railston?" Heffner called querulously.

"You want him, you get him," she retorted and flounced out of the room, leaving the door open to admit fresh air, tangy with the smell of the ocean.

Heffner took too long in deciding to follow her and was not halfway to the door when the entrance from the saloon was suddenly wide and the fat, nightshirted owner stood there, pointing a double-barrel shotgun. He took in the scene at a glance.

"Hold it," he commanded, and Heffner froze.

The salty air began to revive Edge and the barked command cut through the final veils of unconsciousness. He groaned, rolled over on to his back and started to sit up. It felt as if his skull was vibrating.

"I said hold it!" the saloon owner yelled, swinging the shotgun to draw a bead on Edge. "What happened here?"

Edge shook his head to try to clear it. Splinters of glass showered from his hair. Heffner gained confidence now that the shotgun was not pointed towards him.

"Murder!" he exclaimed and waved a shaking hand towards Edge. "He was dealing crooked and Drew Shelby spotted it. He blasted Shelby, then the Eden kid."

Edge spat on the floor and was about to argue. But then he saw the saloon owner's flabby face begin to shake and his small eyes widen in a mixture of apprehension and shock.

"Chadwick Eden was playing poker in my place?" His voice was rasping.

"We didn't know who he was till the final deal," Heffner defended.

Edge struggled to regain full command of his thought processes and to make sense of the fear generated by Eden's presence in the Royal Flush. It was as if the boy's death were of secondary importance to the place in which he had died.

"What was the shooting?" The speaker was a woman. She was behind the bulky figure of the saloon owner, shielded by him.

"Go and get Red Railston," the fat man ordered.

"At this time of night?" The woman sounded incredulous.

"So he won't like it," the fat man said impatiently. "He'll like it even less when you tell him Chadwick Eden's just been shot. Do like I say, Sarah."

Edge spat again and got to his feet, moving slowly to avoid panicking the fat man into any dangerous action. "Was Eden some kind of tin god in these parts?" he asked.

"Gold," the saloon owner answered. "Twenty-two carat solid."

"He bleeds like a mortal man," Edge pointed out sourly, exploring his head for signs of cuts. There were none.

"Just like your neck'll snap at the end of a rope."

Edge pursed his narrow lips. "You hold the trial while I was sleeping?"

The fat man drew in his breath and shook his head slowly. His expression seemed to hold sympathy for Edge. "Mister, you killed Lydia Eden's son. If they had every man in the state of California on a jury, she could afford to buy them all."

"What if I could prove Shelby shot him?"

The flabby cheeks rippled in another negative gesture. "No good. Shelby looks dead to me."

"He is."

"Can't hang a dead man, feller. And there ain't nothing going to satisfy Lydia Eden except the sight of a man swinging at the end of a rope."

Edge turned slightly to look at Heffner. The dapper

little man saw the ice in the blue eyes and the dull sheen of white teeth between slightly parted lips. He recognized the expression as a silent threat and stepped back a pace. His lips trembled. "What happened?" Edge asked softly.

Heffner swallowed hard. "I'll tell it at the trial," he rasped.

"Like it was?"

"Like I have to." He couldn't hold Edge's steady gaze.

"What happened to the woman?"

There seemed to be something of intense interest on the floor. Heffner shuffled his feet and riveted his attention on it. "What woman?"

Edge sighed and sat down on the chair Shelby had vacated. He looked at the fat man in the doorway. "Appears San Francisco is turning into a ghost town," he muttered.

"What?" the fat man asked.

"Forget it. Like he forgot her."

"Heffner would remember a woman," the saloon owner said. "He likes women."

"That's what I thought," Edge said. "And this one was real pin-up material."

CHAPTER TWO

Edge guessed Railston was a big man when he heard the heavy footfalls in the quiet saloon, one stride to every two of the woman who had been sent to fetch

17

the marshal. And he was able to judge something of the man's nature from the way the trembling saloon owner hurried into the back room to allow entrance to Railston.

"He did it, Red!" Heffner wailed, raising an accusing finger towards Edge. "He blasted Lydia Eden's little boy."

The malodorous kerosene lamp swayed at the end of its supporting chain, seemingly with vibration from Railston's anger but perhaps from a draught of ocean air through the rear door. Railston carried a Henry repeating rifle and he swung it towards Edge with the deliberate manner of one intent upon summary execution. But then he halted, feet apart, and stared with deep malevolence at the accused man.

"You just bought enough trouble for ten thousand men, feller," he said with quiet hatred.

Edge cracked his lips in a cold grin. "Into every life a little rain must fall."

Railston was surprised by the lightness in Edge's tone and it was obvious he had come to the Royal Flush expecting to find a cowering murderer. If the marshal had been raised from his bed, he slept in his clothes, for he was fully dressed, his better than six feet frame clothed in a predominantly light grey garb of pants, shirt and buckskin jacket. His boots were black, and so was the kerchief at his neck. The ring on the kerchief and the buttons on his jacket as well as the ornamentation on his boots seemed to be made of gold. As was the five-pointed star in a circle pinned to the left lapel of his jacket. In addition to the Henry, he was armed with two Manhattan Navy Model single-action revolvers, one hanging low on each thigh. Although the marshal was some two inches shorter than Edge, he had a lot more bulk which seemed to be built of muscle at the shoulders and chest, but of softer material at his belly. His nickname

18

came from the long, but well-trimmed hair that topped his large, bullet head and spilled down his bulbous cheeks, just failing to reach the corners of his mouth. His features were cut from a similar but larger pattern to Edge's, a fusion of handsomeness and cruelty presenting varying aspects to different people. But the skin was pale and there was in the green eyes the hint of a coward lurking behind the bravado of a badge. He spoke with a slight accent which suggested Irish parents.

"The sun has sure gone down for you, feller," Railston said, shaking his head.

"I'm beginning to get the impression it shone out of the kid's ass."

Heffner was getting braver by the moment. He giggled.

"On your feet," Railston demanded, jerking the Henry.

Edge complied, noticing for the first time that Railston had not come to the Royal Flush alone. A slight, youngish-looking man stood in the shadows of the doorway, the tinny glint of a deputy's badge in the area of his left breast.

"Take care of the cadavers, Vic," Railston told him, without taking his steady gaze off Edge. "Turn around, feller."

Edge began to do so, slowly.

"Who's going to tell Mrs. Eden?" the saloon owner asked nervously.

The question distracted Railston for a moment and as he shot an angry glance towards the fat man, the rifle wavered. Edge interrupted his turning motion and launched himself into a sudden dive across the floor, his right hand stretching out and closing over the butt of the fallen Colt. He rolled onto his back and threw his body into a sitting position, the

19

revolver aimed steadily at a point two inches below Railston's gold badge.

"You want me to find out if you've got any heart, marshal?" Edge murmured softly.

The deputy had advanced into the room and snapped out a revolver in a fast draw. The shotgun and rifle were aimed in the same direction.

"Don't shoot!" Railston screamed and from the harsh looks he gave his deputy and the fat man it was obvious he wasn't talking to Edge.

The saloon owner actually lowered his gun and it almost slipped from his trembling fingers. But the deputy held his aim steady.

"Lydia wouldn't want him dead," Railston elaborated and from this Edge realized just how strong was the power wielded by Chadwick Eden's mother. Railston was less afraid for his own life than of the anger of the woman.

"You haven't got a chance," the young deputy said evenly.

"More than in a courtroom," Edge answered.

The coolness of Vic's expression seemed to be on the point of breaking up, like ice splintering under the pick, as he considered the validity of Edge's argument. But he held it together.

"You could get Red," he said. "But I'll get you."

Edge showed his teeth, like chips of polished chalk in the darkness of the corner. "Mrs. Eden wouldn't like that."

Vic's eyes flicked for a split second towards Railston, but it was long enough for the contempt to rise to the surface and be seen. "She doesn't own *me*," he said.

Heffner gasped, like a soul-deep Christian who had just heard blasphemy.

Edge kept the Colt trained upon Railston as he spoke. "This gun has fired one shell," he said softly. "I killed Shelby in self-defence. He pulled a pepperbox. It's under the table. His shell ricocheted off the lamp and hit Eden. Heffner won't tell it like that. A whore named Emmeline Greer was here. Find her and get her to talk."

"I'll find her," Vic said and although Edge was not looking at him, he heard enough in the tone to demand trust.

Edge climbed carefully to his feet, maintaining his concentration upon the stoically enraged Railston. Then he suddenly reversed the Colt and tossed it underarm towards the deputy. "Check the load," he invited.

"I'll take that!" Railston snarled, sidestepping over to Vic and snatching the Colt from the young man's grasp. "It's evidence."

Anger flared within Edge, but he checked it. He had made his play and put his trust in the only man who seemed to be beyond the powerful influence of Lydia Eden. And he also knew that no serious harm would come to him until they put a rope around his neck. Paradoxically, he had the woman to thank for that.

"Here's Shelby's gun, Red," Heffner said excitedly, leaning down to reach beneath the table and handing the small pepperbox to the marshal.

Railston grinned evilly and turned his back on his deputy as he checked the chambers. Then he looked at Edge and his grin brightened, emphasizing the evil within him. "Looks to me that your iron fired twice and Shelby's is as clean as a whistle, feller."

Edge spat. "You ought to have been a locomotive engineer, marshal," he said softly. "You're a railroading expert."

It was apparent from the deputy's expression that he agreed with the opinion. But Vic said nothing: just kept pointing his big Colt-Walker at Edge. Railston put down the two guns on the baize.

"Turn around, feller," Railston ordered. "And no sudden moves this time. Fatso, if he so much as blinks, give him both barrels in the knees."

Heffner giggled. "Then he won't have a leg to stand on."

Nobody else laughed as Edge turned around, aware of the saloon owner's nervousness. Railston moved up behind him, holding the Henry easily in one hand as he drew a revolver. For a moment he was in both lines of fire, but Edge wasn't prepared to take the risk. The Colt swung, butt first, and crunched agonizingly upon the same spot where the woman had smashed the bottle. Edge pitched down hard, his forehead smashing into the wall. But there was no pain from the second impact because the blood-red mist had already blotted out the world.

"He would have gone quiet, Red," Vic accused.

"But now he ain't got no choice," Railston came back, holstering his gun, and swinging the Henry up to rest across his shoulder. "I run the law in this part of the city. And you remember that, Paxton. And you be respectful towards Mrs. Eden."

Vic Paxton holstered his own revolver and refused to meet the marshal's steady, angry glare.

"You goin' to tell Lydia, Red?" Fatso asked.

Railston turned his anger towards the saloon owner. "Yeah, I'm going to tell her," he yelled. "After you and Heffner have carried this lousy killer down to the jailhouse. And I'm going to have to tell her that Chad was shot during a poker game in your saloon. Looks like you're finished in this town, Fatso."

The fat man began to tremble so much that the shotgun slipped from his fingers. Saliva trickled from the corner of his mouth and cut a course through the stubble on his many chins. In the saloon his wife, Sarah, began to sob.

"I didn't know Chad was here," he blubbered.

"And I didn't know it was the kid I was playing," Heffner put in, his voice pitched high.

Railston snorted and gathered up the pepperbox and Edge's Colt. He nodded towards the unmoving form of the unconscious man. "Move him," he ordered.

"I ain't dressed," Fatso protested.

"You don't look any better when you are," Railston countered and jerked his head again. The two men went forward to do his bidding. "You take care of the dead men, Paxton," he said harshly to his deputy. "Get the mortician down here to make the arrangements. Lydia Eden will probably want something special for the kid."

"You figure the stranger did it, Red?" Paxton asked.

Heffner and Fatso had hoisted Edge between them and were carrying him through the doorway. "You ever see a feller look more like a killer?" Railston asked, prodding the Henry across the front of Heffner's body, halting him.

The marshal and deputy looked down into the unconscious face of Edge. Even in repose it was possible to see the years of violence and killing etched deeply into the darkened skin.

"He sure don't look like any Sunday school teacher, does he?" Heffner suggested.

Paxton nodded his agreement with that, and Heffner and his fellow beast of burden were allowed to go out into the saloon. Railston shot a final warning glance at Paxton and followed in their wake. Paxton stood where he was for several moments, listening to the sobs of Sarah from the saloon; feeling the anger rise within him. It was visible in an expression that rested easily on his good-looking young face, for he was well-practised in the experience of frustration that had no outlet.

He had spent all of his twenty-two years in this section of San Francisco and his entire working life as a deputy in the office of a corrupt lawman. Another youngster with the same high ideals but a lack of patience would have moved on long ago, in search of less barren territory on which to sow the seeds of honest law and order. But Paxton's strength was in his roots and they were firmly implanted in the city by the ocean. It was, basically, a good and beautiful city and the people in it were, for the most part, decent and honest. He had therefore chosen to stay and do what he could to triumph his ideals over the powerful corrupting influences which had their fountainhead in Lydia Eden and were manifested in the iron rule of Red Railston. And having made the choice, he required all his strength and patience to bide his time.

He was a fresh-faced young man, but there was nothing about his open, even proportioned features that suggested weakness. He had brown, well-trimmed hair with no sideburns or moustache. His eyes were widely set, an open and intelligent blue. His cheekbones were high, his jawline firm and his mouth full of lip. He stood less than six feet, but his frame was solid and, when he had to, he had a speed of movement and quickness of reflex that had surprised many larger men who had provoked him with confidence.

As he conquered his anger at Railston's methods and began to move about the room, his ever-watchful eyes missed nothing. He noted the bullet-scarred baize which indicated the positions of Edge and Shelby, the dent in the lamp where a bullet had been deflected, the shards of glass from a broken bottle, the utter lack of bills among the scattering of cards. And his nostrils caught the faint aroma of a heady perfume, the last remnants of which still remained to be wafted away by the soft breeze off the Pacific. Then he checked Shelby's inert body and found nothing of interest. But the side pocket of Eden's well-cut, expensive jacket was more productive. As he delved a hand inside, Paxton thought he had found a dozen or so silver dollars, but when he brought them out he saw he had been mistaken.

They were the same size as coins, but seemed to be made of bronze. In the center of each was a dollar sign and the figure five. Around the edge was inscribed the legend: GOOD FOR ONE SCREW. Paxton counted them and discovered Eden had bought fifty dollars worth of time with the woman. He put one in his own pocket and returned the remainder to Eden.

Then he went out into the darkened saloon, not sure whether the time had come to make his stand against Railston and the rule of Lydia Eden; but hopeful. Sarah had drained herself dry of tears and was sitting at a table, very erect, as if in a trance. Her eyes seemed dead in their sockets as they followed Paxton's easy progress across the empty saloon.

"Mr Paxton?" she called as he was about to push through the bats-wing doors.

He halted and looked back. "Yes, Sarah," he anticipated. "Mrs Eden really can run you out of the city if she has a mind to seek more revenge than hanging a man."

"I know," the drained woman answered. "I was going to ask you. Will you take in Mint Julep? He'll be more comfortable in one of the cells."

He looked where she was looking and saw what seemed to be a pile of rags on the floor at one end of the bar. He sighed and moved across to the man, sleeping peacefully in a drunken stupor.

"We must have the quietest town drunk in the Far

25

West," he said, showing his wiry strength in the ease with which he tossed the unconscious man over his shoulder.

"He'll miss this place when we're closed up," Sarah said plaintively. "He was always sure of an hour pushing broom here."

Paxton wanted to tell her not to worry, but the slight store of self-confidence he had generated in the back room was already beginning to ebb. For the dirty grey of a new dawn was lightening the darkness of the night out in the street. Alone in the dark hours the mind is capable of triumphing over the greatest adversity: but in the cold light of a new day the harshness of reality calls upon a man for more than the tenuous abstraction of the mere desire to do what is right. So he held his silence as he carried the sleeping drunk out of the saloon and crossed to the opposite sidewalk to thud a fist against the glass door of the undertaker's parlor. The funereal oldtimer was by turns angry at being aroused so early, shocked by the fact of two violent deaths, and delighted to learn that he would have the profitable privilege of handling the arrangements for Chadwick Eden's interment.

When Paxton reached the jail behind the courthouse he found it was empty, save for the still unconscious Edge who was sprawled carelessly upon the straw mattress in the strongest cell. The young deputy put Mint Julep in the adjacent cell, then sat down in Railston's comfortable swivel chair behind the large oak desk. He turned up the wick in the lamp and took out the token he had removed from Chadwick Eden's body, studying it intently as he held it in the circle of his thumb and index finger.

In his cell, Edge did not move. But his subconscious was aware of the abrupt brightening of the light level. It received this as a kind of signal and triggered an impulse into the forefront of the inert mind. Edge's eyes snapped open and immediately reacted to a great bolt of pain that exploded behind them. The lids fell back as the mind refused to accept the agony of awareness and the man's physical body was forced involuntarily down into the depths of insensitive unconsciousness. But in the split-second when they had been focussed upon the world outside, the retinas of the eyes had been imprinted with a face that was familiar but which did not at once register into a pattern of memory. And the mind was no longer allowed to lay dormant for the face was part of a nightmare and there could be no waking until the veils of the past were ripped aside and the memory placed in its proper context.

CHAPTER THREE

The bloody battle of Shiloh was over and although Captain Josiah C. Hedges had learned from an official briefing that the total losses to both the Union and Rebel armies exceeded twenty thousand men he could feel nothing more than a mild sense of anger at the wretched uselessness of the war. He had survived, and whatever fatalities had decimated his cavalry troop were caused through no fault of his. He had come to terms with the war, seeing himself in the role of a man with a job to do. And the job was to kill the enemy and to survive in order to kill more of them. Shiloh, like every other battle and each skirmish in which he had been engaged, had served to prove him able in the task and taught him new ways to be better at it.[*]

The summer of 1862 had run its course and throughout the ungentle autumn that followed there were rumors of the war coming to an end. Few placed any credence in the stories, accepting them for what they were: desperate fantasies called up by miserable minds to act as props to sagging morale in the cold, shortening days. But every man needed hope and it was the desire to see some grain of truth in the rumors that kept them proliferating.

"I hear there's going to be a truce starting Christmas Day," Roger Bell said to Bill Seward as the cavalry troop picked its slow way down a rutted, frozen trail on a hillside in central Tennessee.

They were both young troopers who might have grown up to be honest, hard-working farmers had not the United States erupted into civil war. Now they had been aged and embittered by the fighting and the future would never be good enough for them, because underlying their disenchantment with the war was the knowledge that killing came easy. And their bitterness was created out of the fact that after each murderous encounter with the enemy they had gained nothing. They had joined the Union cause without a cause of their own except perhaps to search for adventure. But the adventure had turned sour because achievement, if such existed, was experienced solely by the staff generals who were able to move a map marker back or forth at the conclusion of each battle. So they grew visibly older every time they killed and with the hardening of their hearts there came a strengthening of their determination to put their newly-acquired skills to good use when the time was ripe.

[*]See: *Edge #4, Killer's Breed.*

Seward gathered his cape around him and shivered, watching his breath turn into white mist in the icy air. "You just made that up, Rog," he complained, his voice a whine, hopeful of a denial.

Bell spat and the spittle froze solid as it hit the hard ground. "It's a nice, warm idea, ain't it, Billy?"

Riding at the head of the column, Hedges could hear the conversation and was on the point of turning in the saddle and ordering the men into silence. But he held his peace. He decided that if a man was stupid enough to imagine he could keep warm with his own thoughts, then he should be allowed the privilege of his luck.

The cavalry column was part of a 45,000-strong army under William S. Rosecrans, marching south from Nashville towards the town of Murfreesboro where, according to intelligence reports, some 40,000 rebels were camped. The weather had been deteriorating ever since the massive army had set out and there were no signs of a let-up in the freezing conditions.

"It's December 31, lunkhead!" The harsh words came from Frank Forrest, the sergeant of the troop. War had not aged him because he had tasted killing long before the opening of hostilities, bounty hunting for renegades in the Arizona Territory. He was a big, mean-looking man with a crooked mouth and the unwavering stare of aggressiveness. It was, perhaps, a measure of the man's ill-directed strength of character that he was able to keep track of time while to so many others the passage of the days had lost any meaning.

"I didn't say what Christmas, Sarge," Bell came back after a few moments of hesitation.

Seward giggled.

"Shut your smart mouth!" Forrest commanded and the troop was driven into silence.

Hedges allowed himself a small grin at his own wisdom in promoting Forrest to the non-com rank. For the most part, he had a first-class troop in the context of the kind of war they were fighting. But the nucleus of the group was formed of six men who were potential troublemakers. Like Bell and Seward, Hal Douglas, John Scott and Bob Rhett were youngsters who had grown to enjoy killing but resent the lack of reward for it. They were expert fighters, but lacked discipline. However, they did possess an ill-conceived respect for Forrest, the professional killer, and Hedges had capitalized upon this by giving the older man his ranking. And Forrest, with the instinct for survival that was an integral requisite of his former profession, was a hard taskmaster in his demands for obedience. But, of course, his usefulness in the role was dependent upon the opinion he held of his commanding officer, and Hedges was constantly aware that one mistake by him could crack the uneasy rapport he had with Forrest.

Almost as if he was aware that he was the subject of the captain's thoughts, Forrest urged his horse up alongside Hedges' mount.

"We been a long time without a fight, Captain," Forrest said absently, looking ahead into the gloom of the winter evening, at the line of blue-uniformed horse soldiers and infantry snaking down the hillside.

Hedges gave Forrest a sidelong glance and saw the impatient belligerence in the ugliness of his profile. "Shiloh ought to have been enough for any man in one year," he said.

Forrest turned a grin towards Hedges. The teeth were stained dark brown by tobacco. "It's New Year's Eve."

"So let's wait until tomorrow," Hedges suggested.

"It's going to be a cold night."

There was shouting ahead and both men looked in

that direction and saw the column begin to break into two, then four, then six lines; spreading out in an uneven formation across a broad front where the slope of the hillside flattened out and gave way to a wide expanse of cotton fields.

"Looks like Rosecrans figures things are going to warm up, sir," Forrest suggested laconically.

Messengers whipped their horses up the treacherous hillside with vapor billowing from their nostrils and those of their mounts. One skidded to a halt facing Hedges and threw up a clumsy salute. Hedges ordered his troopers to pause.

"Message from the general commanding, sir," the messenger said breathlessly. "Scouts have spotted the enemy making ready a mile across the cotton fields. You're to take your troop on to the right flank and lead the infantry under the artillery barrage."

Hedges nodded his acknowledgement of the order and the messenger went off at a gallop, scattering groups of men who were already trying to take up positions issued by harrassed officers.

"Oh, Christ!" Douglas yelled. "Under the goddam artillery. Them stupid clods are likely to drop their shot on top of us."

"At least that would keep you quiet!" Forrest yelled at him.

"Move them out to the right," Hedges ordered and kept his horse reined to an uneasy standstill as Forrest wheeled away, his arm raised to beckon the troopers in his wake.

Douglas, who was probably the worst corporal in the Union Army, was still complaining—although in lower tones—as he and Scott rode after Forrest. Seward and Bell were next, their expressions animated by the need for action. The rest of the troopers streamed along behind, an uneven mixture of old and young, large and small, stupid and intelligent. But all had one thing in common—they were afraid. This had to be, because death was waiting less than a mile away and none could know who it would strike. However, the fear visible in each man's face was as different from the next man's as were his features. Thus, while one man allowed his horse to find the way as he read from the Bible, another was calling softly to his mother. An old regular soldier was thinking about his wife. A boy who looked as if he had never shaved was recalling the occasion he could have slept with his girl but didn't. And interspersed among these men, who had something precious to lose, were those like Bell and Seward for whom the past was as non-existent as the future. But nothing was as empty as death, and in the calm before the battle even such men as these had to look inwards and acknowledge the dark presence of fear.

Such a man as Joe Hedges, too, for although he had been honed as hard as any man by his experiences, he did have a future, being tenderly preserved for him by a kid brother on an Iowa farm. Whether he could face that future if the time came, he did not know. But he did know that Jamie was relying on him, and this was at the root of Hedges' fear as he urged his horse forward.*

"Say one for me, trooper," he said as he rode past the soldier with the Bible.

"It's for all of us, sir," the man said.

Hedges reached the end of the line where Forrest was blowing on his clasped hands as he peered into the gloom. "Can't see a thing out there except cotton," he said sourly.

"Don't you believe our scouts?" Hedges asked him.

Forrest began to rub his hands together as he

*See: Edge #1, The Loner.

grinned. "I've stayed alive by not believing anything I haven't seen for myself."

Edge returned the grin. "That's a lot of open field down there. Like to go and see for yourself?"

The artillery began to move through the lines, the gunners cursing at the horses to speed up the movement of the big brass smoothbore cannon to the hastily prepared emplacements at the edge of the field. Behind them rolled the flatbeds low on their springs with the twelve-pound shot and slug cannisters.

"The rebs are the guys in grey," Seward taunted one of the struggling gunners who had to use all his strength to prevent his cannon side-sliding on ice into a small gulley.

The man stared hatefully up at the arrogant youngster. "You're safe," he retorted sourly. "Whoever saw a dead cavalryman?"

A large group of infantry waiting behind Hedges' troop raised a sardonic cheer for the gunner's remark.

"Hell, you're just plain jealous of our skills," Bell shouted at the foot soldiers. "We're the cream of the army."

"Goddam cream puffs!" a voice called from out of the gloom.

Bell, Seward, Scott and Douglas kicked loose of a stirrup and prepared to slide from their saddles.

"Stay in 'em!" Forrest roared, his voice cutting across the laughter of the foot soldiers. "Save it for the rebs."

Once again, Forrest's harsh voice and menacing demeanor held the men's anger in check. He continued to glower at the mounted soldiers until their rage at the insult had died.

"Guess word about Rhett has spread," Hedges put in lightly.

"I hear he's on the mend, sir," Forrest replied.

Hedges sighed. "Maybe we'll be lucky. Maybe some other troop will get him."

33

Bob Rhett was a New England dandy who'd been wounded in mysterious circumstances during the Shenandoah Valley campaign. He was a coward with homosexual tendencies but had held his place in the troop's central group because the others found him amusing. But in Hedges' book the man was a no-account fag who disgraced the uniform he wore.

"Hey, we're moving," a cavalryman called, and Hedges looked with the others down the slope to where cavalry and infantry were beginning to push between the cannon, out into the cotton fields.

"Let's go give them hell!" another voice encouraged, sadly lacking in the confidence the words had intended to exude.

Across the darkness the enemy cannon opened up with far-off splashes of bright orange along a wide front. Hurried orders were yelled by officers and noncoms and whether it had been the intention or not, the Union lines moved forward, shouting in a mixture of fear and blood lust. Not for the first time in the war, Hedges saw the battle plan of a general overruled by the panicked actions of the moment as officers forgot or muddled their orders amid the clamor of undisciplined troops impatient to be done with the fighting. As Hedges understood it, Rosecrans had wanted to hold with his right flank and attack with his left. But the sudden bombardment towards the right was triggering an immediate response. Instead of advancing and holding, the great mass of men were spilling down the hill and streaming far into the expanse of frozen cotton fields. And as the murderous hail of cannon shot began to smash into the foot of the hill it was obvious that only the bravest of the brave would be prepared to hold the line. It was a simple question of advance or withdraw, for to be brave in such a situation was to show mindless stupidity.

"Forward!" Hedges yelled and heeled his mount into

a downhill gallop as somewhere far off a corps bugler sounded the charge.

The Union battery opened up then, sending shot whistling through the freezing air towards the bright flashes of the rebels' second fusillade. The night was almost full-born now and the wispy patterns of a tenuous mist trailed across the fields, cleanly white before it became contaminated by the evil greyness of gunpowder smoke. Out amongst it, brushing through the cold stiffened stalks of cotton, men and horses pressed forward, some at the run and others with circumspection: all keeping low.

More than a hundred Union men were already dead, twisted and bleeding along the line of cannon emplacements. By luck, for there had been no time to allow judgment, the rebel gunners had zeroed directly in on the Union's leading line and a mixture of ball shot and lead pellet cannisters had wrought their own particular brand of havoc.

One man's head had been wrenched from his shoulders by a ball. Another lay face down as if still a complete man, but as a wailing friend turned him over the entire front of his body was a mass of blood-soaked lacerations from flying pellets. Two gunners were trapped beneath an overturned cannon, one with a smashed skull from where the barrel had hit him, the other impaled through the stomach by a snapped-off spoke.

As Hedges galloped forward, his mind was impervious to the sight of the mutilated corpses and the terrible cries of the wounded. He was concerned solely with the able and the living for upon them depended the outcome of the battle and this was all that mattered.

"We lost our line to heaven!" Scott shouted with high excitement as a twelve-pounder whistled in and a man screamed.

Hedges glanced to his left through eyes narrowed against the rush of icy air and saw a book arcing away into the night. The arm of the man who had held it spun off on a lower trajectory. The trooper who had been praying for the whole army continued to scream as he stared down at the blood-soaked patch on his shoulder where his arm had been ripped off. Then he tumbled from his horse, which raced ahead and kicked over backwards, taking a second ball shot full in the chest.

"Somebody up there didn't like him," Billy Seward yelled, ducking as another shot whistled in and burrowed through the chest of an already dead infantryman.

The troop was in amongst the trampled cotton now and they could hear small-arms fire ahead, frail sounding against the pounding roar of the artillery barrages. The mist with its interlacing of acrid gunsmoke was thickening and Hedges slowed the pace, concerned at the danger of smashing through the Union infantry. He unbooted the Henry and all along the line the troopers took out their motley selection of single-shot and repeating weapons, breech and muzzle-loaders. The metal frames of the guns were cold to the touch, but warm in the comfort of self-protection they offered.

Two men came running out of the mist and a trooper sent a bullet humming towards them. It crackled harmlessly into the downtrodden cotton stalks.

"Don't shoot!" one of the men screamed. "Union."

The second man couldn't speak. His jaw had been shot away. His teeth looked very white against the scarlet pulp of his fleshless chin. Hedges' voice rasped an order to hold fire as he reined in his horse. The cannon had ceased to fire, each battery commander unsure of how far his own advance had progressed and unwilling to risk dropping shot upon his comrades. Behind the curtain of wavering mist the crackle of rifle and revolver fire was suddenly loud and deadly. The warcries of bravado merged with the screams of the wounded in a terrifying stridency that spooked men and horses alike.

"Go back!" the uninjured man implored. "There's a million of 'em. Go back! They're murdering us."

"How far?" Hedges demanded.

The man waved inconclusively towards the racket of the battle. "Back there. It's slaughter."

The man with no jaw made a groaning sound, but no pain showed in his glazed eyes. His companion looked at him with great compassion, then reached out and took his hand. When he turned back to look up at Hedges, there were tears streaming down his face.

"It's my son," he said. "He was a real handsome boy. We've had enough. "We're going home to mother."

He took one step into a run and then the back of his head exploded under the impact of two heavy caliber bullets. Four men in Confederate grey broke into the open, two of them with smoking muskets. Forrest and Hedges fired together and the two rebels with primed guns crumpled, pouring blood from chest wounds. The man with no jaw whirled and threw himself at his father's killers. He died with them, under a hail of bullets from the troopers that riddled all three bodies.

A snarl burst from Hedges and he turned in the saddle to deliver a tonguelashing to his men. But before he could start, the thud of running feet and the whistling of bullets changed the order of priorities.

"It ain't the whites of their eyes we want to see!" he yelled, experiencing a familiar rise of excitement within his chest.

"Just make sure the bastards are wearing grey!" Forrest augmented.

37

Thirty guns were brought up and aimed into the mist. Thirty fingers curled around triggers and thirty eyes narrowed behind back sights. Thirty horses smelt the fear and excitement of their riders and blew their vaporized breath into the chill of the night.

Hedges nerve was as cold and steady as the steel frame of the Henry. As he listened to the running feet and the crack of gunfire, he recalled Shiloh and the shattering self-discovery he had made during the battle. There, amid the bloodbath, he had learned how to kill without compunction and glory in the sight of men falling by his hand. There, surrounded by death at its most horrible, he had found exhilaration in killing. And now, as he waited in this new arena, he was aware of the same high excitement. The farm in Iowa and everything it represented was smothered by the glory of this moment. Shiloh had not been an isolated incident. *He wants to win the damn war all on his own!* Bell had shouted at the height of the battle and Hedges knew this was true. He wanted to kill and kill and not stop until he had blasted the life from every last man in a Confederate uniform.

The soldiers in blue came through first, breathless and pale-faced, some trailing blood. Without breaking their hurried retreat, they veered to left and right to thread between the line of nervous horses. Many moved like mindless puppets, as if led by cords towards the safety of the Union lines. A few stared up into the faces of the cavalrymen with eyes that poured scorn upon a tactic they considered reckless to the point of stupidity.

"Get the bastards!" Forrest yelled and thirty shots rang out.

The line of rebels had emerged from the mist at the run, their faces jubilant as they leapt across the Union dead and gave chase to the retreating troops. More than a score died before their minds could realize the tragedy of victory becoming the ultimate defeat. Six more writhed on the prickly, cold ground with agonizing wounds as the remainder got off shots, toppling dead and injured troopers from their mounts.

"Hit the dirt!" Hedges roared and the troopers slid from their saddles, firing on the move into the fresh wave of rebels which seemed to materialize from the mist as if born from it. As horses lost their riders they either collapsed into death throes or bolted forward, trampling the dead and wounded and sending other men crashing to the ground under flying hooves.

"They're holding!" a rebel voice called through the gunfire. "Down, down, down!"

The mist seemed suddenly to exhaust its supply of grey-clad figures as the rebels halted their headlong advance and threw themselves to the ground, below the hail of bullets sent puncturing through the darkness from the smoking muzzles of the cavalrymen's guns.

"Forward on your belly," Hedges murmured to Forrest and started to move, levering himself along on his elbows, wincing as the sharp, broken stalks prodded his arms.

Forrest whispered the order to the next man and the message trickled down the line. They fired as they went and only stopped when they reached the pile of bodies, Union mixed with rebel. The firing died down on this section of the battleline as both sides took time to reload and to free jammed weapons. Far off, gunfire clattered and men cried out. The mist made it sound as if the din came from another world.

"Jesus!" Scott yelled as he rested his forehead on the ground, expecting its feverishness to be cooled by the frost that had laid a sparkling cloak over the field. Instead he felt the sticky warmth of blood which had spilled from three holes in the stomach of a rebel.

"Yes, my son!" a voice thundered from the rebel line.

"I knew he was on our side!" a young voice yelled and a burst of laughter shattered into the stillness. Hedges had loaded ten rounds into the Henry. He snapped home the magazine and began to squeeze the trigger and pump the action, waving the rifle to left and right. Screams of pain and cries of alarm greeted each new shot.

Other troopers followed the captain's lead, then buried their heads under their arms as answering fire cracked and bullets whistled towards them. Three troopers died and two more collapsed with non-fatal wounds. Another stared fixedly at a dead comrade for long seconds, then pulled himself erect, turned and ran. Hedges rolled over on to his back and sighted the rifle along his body.

"Hold it, trooper!" he roared.

The man didn't hear him. Hedges squeezed the trigger and saw blood spurt from the center of the blue back.

"Unarmed and in the back!" a voice said bitterly from down the line.

"Man runs under fire, he gets it any way we can give it!" Forrest retorted.

"If I figure an explanation's needed, I'll give it," Hedges snapped.

Forrest grinned and executed a mocking salute in the prone position. "Beg the Captain's pardon."

Hedges caught a movement ahead and snapped off a shot. A wounded rebel had been playing dead and thought he saw an opportunity to scuttle away to safety. The bullet took him high in the cheek and sprayed blood from the top of his head. The rebels retaliated with a burst of concentrated fire that pinned the troopers flat to the ground. When it ceased abruptly, no man made a move to back away.

"One of us had an effect on them," Forrest muttered.

Hedges spat onto the solid ground. "An illustration is worth a thousand words, Sergeant," he answered.

There was a rustling sound ahead and the troopers tensed themselves to combat a charge, raising and levelling their guns across the slumped forms of the dead. But instead of increasing, the sound diminished and was soon lost amid the far-off crackling of small arms fire on another section of the front.

"Hey, the rebs are pulling back," Bell whispered.

"Yeah," Seward agreed. "Let's go chase them all the way to Richmond."

"What about it, Captain?" Forrest asked.

Hedges shook his head. "How many shells you got left, Sergeant?"

Forrest checked his ammunition pouch, and the other troopers realized the importance of the query and did likewise.

"That's what makes you officer material," Forrest allowed. "Ten shots plus what's in my iron and then I'm cleaned out."

Groans from along the line told of a similar limit on the fire power of the troop.

"You called it right again, sir," Scott said.

"Richmond will keep," Seward put in.

"Let's make it slow and easy," Hedges said, easing to his feet, continuing to stare into the mist.

The troopers did the same, trigger fingers curled. But the rebel withdrawal had not been a ruse. As the survivors of the troop pulled back, carrying their wounded, there was no surprise onslaught. They walked backwards all the way across the frozen ground from the piles of dead at the scene of the skirmish to where the broken bodies and smashed cannon of the gun emplacements were.

"The crud ran out on us!" a trooper exclaimed angrily as he surveyed the deserted positions.

"So you've learned a lesson about this lousy war," Forrest said sourly. "We might look like one big army when we're lined up for a battle. But when the shooting starts, there's just you and the guys you can see. Every other bastard's taking care of himself."

It took Hedges and his troop two hours to find their own line and the body-littered hillside was tragic evidence of many skirmishes such as the one that had engaged them. The entire right flank of Rosecrans' army had been forced back at a sharp angle to the center and left, which was still clashing with the enemy on the mist-shrouded plain below.

"Hey," a trooper called wearily as the men spotted campfires ahead. "I think it's after midnight."

"You got no glass slipper to lose," Forrest told him acidly. "And that was no ball we were just at."

"But it's New Year's," the man insisted.

Forrest turned to look at Hedges and the two men locked their mean eyes into a single stare. Then the older, bigger man grinned and for the first time ever, Hedges saw genuine humor through the coldness.

"Hope you ain't going to kiss me, Captain," he said.

Hedges allowed the corners of his lips to turn up. "Hope's about all we've got going for us in this war. And for a guy like you, I reckon it springs eternal. Hopeful New Year."

They clasped hands and then Hedges moved among the men to express the same wish to all of them. Even the man who had scorned Hedges for shooting the coward seemed to draw the warmth of fellow feeling from the gesture. And on a night as cold as that, any vestige of warmth was welcome.

*   *   *

A warm San Francisco day was pushing ahead into mid-morning when Edge came fully awake from his unconsciousness and sat on the side of the rough mattress to allow the pain in his head to subside. He could hear a man snoring in the next cell, but when he looked through the bars the grizzled face of the sleeping drunk meant nothing to him. He looked in another direction and saw Vic Paxton regarding him from behind the marshal's desk.

"Headache?" the young deputy inquired. The question seemed to arise more from a desire to be polite than out of concern.

"I've been hurt worse," Edge answered. "The marshal doesn't like to take any chances, does he?"

Paxton grimaced. "He's mean and he's a coward. Mix the two and you come up with something that isn't really human."

The sunlight through the barred window in the outside wall was strong and yellow and seemed to be feeding the pain under Edge's skull. He stood up and turned his back to it. The cell seemed to cant, first to the left, then the right. Edge reached for the bars of the door and leaned against them. After a few moments the world came back onto an even keel.

"Where is he?"

Paxton rubbed his eyes, which were red-rimmed from lack of sleep. "Still out at the Garden of Eden, I guess."

"The what?"

"Lydia Eden's spread at the side of the ocean north of here. Don't you recall what happened last night?"

Edge sighed. "Yeah, I recall. Will they hang me with a serpent from an apple tree?"

Paxton didn't crack a smile. "You'll have a proper trial and if you're found guilty, sentence will be carried out under due process of law."

Edge's expression was impassive. "Should I be grateful for that?"

"Do you want me to fix up a lawyer for you?"

Edge reached around behind himself and felt the flatness of his hip pocket. "I can't afford one. Somebody heisted better than two and a half thousand bucks off me."

Paxton showed his surprise with arched eyebrows. "You won that much playing poker with Shelby and Heffner?"

"I earned it for bringing a woman over the Sierras," Edge answered.* "Maybe it was another woman who took it. Or maybe it was Railston."

"Red gets well paid by Mrs Eden," Paxton said.

"So go find the woman and have her hire me a lawyer," Edge suggested.

Paxton nodded. "I was waiting for you to wake up. Know anything about her?"

Edge sat down on the bed again and massaged the side of his head. "Her name was Emmeline Greer and she looked like a whore. Eden brought her along. For luck, he said. It was bad."

Paxton rose from the desk and approached the cell. He halted beyond reach and took out the token. He held it up and it shone in the sunlight. The light bounced into the face of the drunk and he rolled over and came noisily awake.

"Eden had ten of these on him," the deputy said.

Edge squinted at the token and leaned forward to read the legend inscribed upon it. "Ambitious, wasn't he? They say it all started in the Garden of Eden. I knew what she was. Now I know she was the five-dollar kind."

"You don't know any house in the city that uses these?" Paxton asked earnestly.

Edge shrugged and felt a reassuring weight at the back of his neck. He raised a hand to prod with his fingers beneath the collar of his shirt and felt the

*See: Edge #5, Blood on Silver.

smooth handle of the razor protruding from its pouch. He dropped his hand before Paxton could become suspicious. "I'm a stranger in town," he answered. "And I never pay for it anyway."

"Hey, let me look at that, there."

Both Edge and Paxton turned towards the drunk, who had hauled himself into a sitting position on the bed and was staring with rheumy eyes at the reflective token. He was an old man, painfully thin in his tattered Eastern suit, with a face that was deathly white under the streaks of dirt and several days' growth of stubble. He wiped a dewdrop from the tip of his hawkish nose and sucked at his toothless gums with flaking lips.

"It won't buy you any wine," Paxton told him.

"I know that," the drunk replied in an insulted tone. "It's a pussy pass, ain't it?"

Paxton grinned wearily. "How would you know that? You'd rather have a snort than a screw any day."

"Don't you make fun of me, young Paxton," the drunk chided. "I been around this town ever since the war. And I pushed a broom in more places than the Market Street saloons."

"Places like cathouses?" Edge demanded.

"They get dirty, just like saloons," the drunk pointed out.

"Show it to him," Edge snapped at Paxton.

The deputy moved to the next cell and was not hesitant in approaching the door of this one.

The drunk peered at the token, then nodded emphatically. "Yeah. They charge high, so they pay good. Only trouble, I was falsely accused of doing something to one of the girls. I can't work there no more."

"Work where?" Edge said sharply.

"Real sharp place," the drunk said reflectively. "Plush, you know? Up on Nob Hill where the big money changes hands. Skyline Hotel."

45

Edge forgot about the drunk and narrowed his eyes as he stared at Paxton. The young deputy held the steady gaze, but was glad to have the iron bars in between.

"Railston could make it tough for me," he said.

"You want to stay a deputy all your life?" Edge came back.

Paxton's expression darkened. "You're in no position to force any issues."

Edge shrugged and gave an impression of relaxing, leaning back against the wall. "Okay, I'm used to working out my own problems."

"Don't you ride Deputy Paxton," the drunk muttered aggressively. "This country's built on good, honest men of his kind."

"Sure," Edge snarled. "Because the other kind make the play and bury his kind. And his kind have heads thick enough to make good foundations."

"Don't you pay no heed to him, Mr. Paxton," the drunk urged, glaring at Edge. Then he grinned at the deputy. "You'd be better employed letting me have a snort of Red Railston's whiskey. Just to settle my indigestion, like."

"Shut up, Mint Julep!" Paxton yelled.

"Yeah, shut up," Edge concurred as he stretched out full length on the rancid mattress. Just as the face of the drunk had triggered a memory from the deep past in Edge's unconscious mind, so the name Paxton called him searched for a place in a mind that was awake but numbed by pain.

"What'd you say her name was?" Paxton asked.

"Emmeline Greer," Edge replied, not opening his eyes. "Big boobs and a strong arm."

"You didn't ought to talk about things like that in jail," Mint Julep whined. "Gives a man ideas that ain't no use to him."

"You been in jail a lot?" Edge asked softly, staring into the darkness behind his eyelids.

"More than enough," the drunk said with a sigh. "I'm a regular."

Edge's voice was a snarl. "Then you ought to have the pull to take care of your ideas."

CHAPTER FOUR

The mangled remains of Rosecrans' army moved wearily into the town of Murfreesboro to recover from the effects of the battle and await replacements for its dead and wounded. It had been an odd and an inconclusive clash that to the men in the field appeared as nothing less than wholesale slaughter for nominal gain. It did not finish until late on the night of the second day in the New Year and Braxton Bragg's rebel Army of Tennessee should have dealt the Union a crushing defeat. But, as had happened so often in the tragedy of the Civil War, decisions were taken in the heat of the moment which were totally inexplicable. The rebels successfully pushed the Union's right flank into a staggered line that trailed behind the left and then for an entire day failed to press home the advantage. Sporadic firing was exchanged along the picket lines and then the Union artillery began to bombard the Rebel right as Rosecrans sought to grasp the initiative. Suddenly, under cover of darkness on that second day of a cold January, the

Army of Tennessee withdrew and struck south in full retreat.

But the views of the men in the field were not invited, and neither were the opinions of mere captains. And in truth, once they were settled into the comparative comfort and warmth of what amounted to a rest camp in Murfreesboro, such men as Hedges and his troopers readily accepted their lot of knowing little: and quickly came to care less. Once more, they had survived when so many had been killed or maimed and nothing which had resulted in the overall context of the war could be of more importance than this.

Spring came early that year and many of the men complained that the bone-deep cold they had experienced during the battle was not relieved until the middle of May, after a solid month of day-long sunshine had radiated on to the vast bivouac area on the edge of town.

Replacements flowed in steadily from the north and a supply route was opened to bring in the essentials and some luxuries of army life. It was in the late afternoon of a balmy day towards the end of May when Hedges stood at the mouth of his tent to watch the arrival of another wagon train with the inevitable column of reinforcements straggling along at the rear. Other officers and men off duty, and many of those actively engaged in the routine chores of camp life, watched with varying degrees of interest. Some were thinking of mail from home, others of relatives who could be among the newcomers. Some men wanted nothing more than a fresh supply of tobacco. The vast majority had no other motive for their interest than a desire to see if there were any new whores for the Murfreesboro cathouse.

"You see what I see, sir?" Forrest said, moving up to stand alongside Hedges.

The officer looked at the sergeant and then beyond him, to where the remainder of the troop were grouped, eyes roving hungrily along the wagon train. He was pleased with what he saw, for they were probably the best turned-out soldiers in the camp area. Smartly dressed in brand-new uniforms, with hair cut to a regulation length and with no facial stubble beyond the permitted moustache and sideburns of those who chose to wear them. And they stood proud and erect, even in their mood of relaxation, evidencing the success of the harsh daily drill program Hedges had implemented.

"They'll all have the clap," Hedges answered, looking with faint amusement at a wagon near the end from which a cluster of some fifteen women and girls were waving, and laughing at the ribald comments of the watching soldiers.

"I wasn't meaning them, Captain," Forrest said. "If it affects the eyes, I think I maybe already caught a dose."

Hedges glanced at him, then away, in the direction the sergeant was looking.

"It's just got to be him, hasn't it?" Forrest continued. "Nobody else would have the gall to roll back to his troop like that. But if it's him, what's he doing with a dame?"

Bringing up the rear of the wagons, behind the three-file column of replacements, was a flatbed with a cavalry trooper on the box; and beside him was the slim figure of a girl. Loaded on behind them were several crates which could contain nothing else but whiskey.

Hedges reached into the mouth of the tent and brought out a pair of fieldglasses. He raised them and scanned the length of the train, then focussed in on the back-marking flatbed. The man sitting on the box was tall and slim, young and handsome. He

49

looked well-fed and content with his lot, like some of the men in the column who were new recruits, yet to see their dreams of adventure shattered by the reality of war. But the man on the wagon wasn't a new recruit. Hedges used the binoculars to stare close into the eyes and he saw they were glazed and guessed the reason.

"It's Rhett," Hedges confirmed sourly.

Forrest turned to grin at the men. "Hey, there's a fruit wagon coming in," he yelled. "Bob Rhett's aboard the flatbed at the end."

The comment drew a negative response from the more recent members of the troop, but those who could recall the Shenandoah Valley campaign burst into raucous laughter.

"We all better keep our backs to the wall from now on, men!" Seward yelled in explanation and took several mincing steps to emphasize his meaning to the others.

"He's got some pussy with him," Forrest put in.

"Christ, she won't know which way to turn," Douglas exclaimed to a renewed burst of merriment, louder now that all the men could share the joke. "What's she like, Captain?"

Hedges raised the glasses again, as the wagon train halted in the camp compound: all except the final wagon which pulled out of the line and around the column to head towards the cavalry troopers' quarters. He saw Rhett's face again, grinning now as the man recognized a group of familiar figures, then panned the glasses over to the girl and caught his breath. He tightened his hands around the binoculars to keep them from trembling.

She was in her early twenties and moderately attractive, with an almost pretty face and a figure that was slimly built and hinted at, rather than emphasized, her sexuality. She had large green eyes and long dark hair and her complexion was pale with the merest touch of make-up. Her name was Jeannie Fisher and she had once followed Hedges from Parkersburg to Washington, looking for a boy and finding a man. Now she had found that man for a second time and as Hedges lowered the glasses and she looked into his face her smile told the world how deliriously happy the discovery made her.

The wheels of the flatbed skidded and as the rig slid to a dust-raising halt, Rhett leapt to his feet and threw up an elaborate salute.

"Trooper Rhett reporting for duty, sir," he slurred. "Fit and good as new again."

Hedges responded to the salute without looking at him. He hadn't taken a woman before Jeannie found him in Washington and there had not been one since. As she sat primly beside the swaying Rhett, she was dressed in a modest, high-necked gown, its whiteness streaked with the dust of the trail. But Hedges could recall what lay beneath the concealing fabric and his lower stomach burned with the need to renew his knowledge.

"Hello, Jeannie," he said softly.

"Hello, Captain," she answered.

The men who had crowded around the wagon were grinning stupidly from out of their discomfort. What should have been a bantering reunion with a wounded comrade was smothered by the strangely tender coming together of the officer and the girl. Rhett's New England drawl injected relief into the tension.

"I bring gifts for everyone," he announced. "Whiskey for the rabble and the Captain's lady for the Captain."

Hedges moved forward and held up a hand to assist Jeannie to the ground. "Glad to have you back," he lied to Rhett, then turned to Forrest. "Quarter him,

51

Sergeant. And make sure they don't drown in that redeye."

As Forrest grinned and saluted, Hedges reached up and swung Jeannie's valise off the wagon. Then, as she rested a frail hand on his arm, he walked her off the camp, through the hectic activity of unloading the wagons and assigning the new men to their quarters. There were two hotels in the town, neither of them entirely suitable for an unchaperoned girl. But one was not openly a brothel and Hedges got Jeannie a room there. He specified a double and when they had been shown up, he kicked the door closed and took her roughly in his arms. She remembered him well from Washington and made no protest, submitting meekly, then with an ardor equal to his own as their bodies pressed together and their mouths became fused in a passionate kiss.

"You haven't changed, Joe," she said breathlessly as they at last parted, Hedges dictating the end of the embrace.

"Did you expect me to?" he asked, holding her away from him at arms length so that his hooded eyes could rove over the length of her body.

"I thought there might have been other women," she said, and it was as it had been before: she both loved and feared him at the same time. Loved the complete man that he was, but trembled inwardly at the latent enjoyment of violence that lurked just beneath the surface of his outer shell.

"There weren't," he said.

She smiled, filled with happiness. "I'm glad."

"There wasn't the time," he told her flatly.

The joy was shattered and threatened to spill out as tears. He released her and began to unfasten his uniform buttons.

"Don't you want to know how I came to be here, Joe?" she asked, not looking at him.

52

"Later maybe," he replied, shrugging out of his tunic. "I know why you came."

"Like Washington, you think?" Her voice was soft and infinitely sad.

He nodded and began to remove his shirt. "Like Washington. To get laid."

She flinched. "Isn't there any more to it than that, Joe?"

"Maybe," he allowed. "But everything's got to start someplace. I'm a man and you're a woman. Screwing is a good place for us."

Deep in her heart she had known what it would be like. But on the long journey south from Washington she had not been able to prevent her mind conjuring up romantic fantasies of their meeting: of soft moonlight and gentle courtship, poetic phrases and tender persuasion. But because she loved him so dearly, she surrendered to the reality and shed her clothing with a sudden willingness in the bright, sunlit room. And as she spread her slim, pale nakedness upon the bed and opened her body to his driving hardness, the circumstances ceased to have significance. When she folded her arms and legs about him and he caressed her and thrust into her she loved him with a fierce intensity that was generated by every throbbing fiber of her physical and spiritual being. And as his warmth flowed into her it filled her with a glowing pride because she knew that at that moment in time she owned and had tamed this man.

But then it was gone, as he withdrew from her and rolled on to his back, transforming into the complete man, sufficient to himself.

"How did you get tied up with the fag?" he asked suddenly, staring up at the ceiling, through the floating dust motes spinning in the shaft of sunlight from the window.

"I was working in a recruitment office in the city,"

she replied, her eyes moving up and down along the brown, toughened flesh of his body. "It handled the assigning of the previously wounded, too. When I heard Mr. Rhett was being sent back to your troop, I asked him to bring me with him. Was it as good as before?"

She turned her head on the pillow and he was drawn to look into her face. He could see she desperately wanted him to need her and his lips curled back in a smile. Because she was searching so hard for it, she was able to see a flicker of warmth through the cold blueness of his eyes.

"Like I said," he told her softly, reaching across to rest his forearm atop the warm mounds of her breasts. "It was a good place to start."

This simple contact was enough to arouse a response from deep inside her and there was a complete abandonment of modesty as she sought an intimate meeting point with him. Her expression remained sad.

"When there's a start, there's often an end," she said.

He continued to smile as he fitted his body against hers. "So let's get the end away," he murmured.

They spent the remainder of the afternoon together and he didn't leave to return to the camp until darkness had settled over the town and oil lamps had begun to burn in windows and from within the regular lines of tents. Because of the large size of the resting army and the smallness of Murfreesboro the town was off-limits to the vast majority of men, with the lack of privilege arranged on a rota basis. But each night the town was alive with gaiety as those men with freedom of movement relieved the boredom of camp life by drinking at the three saloons and emptying their lust into the imported whores and those local girls who considered it acceptable or necessary to fraternize with the occupying army.

On the night of the day when Jeannie Fisher came to town, there was a social arranged to be held in the meeting house at the other end of Murfreesboro from where the camp was set up. It was not sponsored by the army, but by the local Presbyterian Church, under the auspices of an idealistic preacher who planned it as a means to combat the degradation of vice and drinking that had gripped Murfreesboro since the soldiers came.

Hedges went to the meeting house with Jeannie for the simple reason that he was not a hard-drinking man and their lovemaking of the afternoon had left him in need of a respite before taking her again. The preacher, a middle-aged man with a rotund build and a round, anxious-looking face had, with his church workers, done the best he could to offer the guests a cheerful environment for their relaxation. There was a three-man band on a stage at one end of the hall, a table loaded with food, another supporting bowls of fruit punch and a third, close to the door, where men were asked to leave their guns. The ceiling was hung with decorations of colored paper, and fresh flowers sprung from vases fixed around the walls.

When Hedges and Jeannie arrived the festivities were already well underway, with both soldiers and local civilians whirling laughing girls in time with the syncopated music supplied by the three sweating musicians.

"Welcome Captain!" the preacher greeted enthusiastically, with a slight bow towards Jeannie. "We're so pleased you could come. We would appreciate it if you will leave your arms with us."

He used the plural because, while he was in front of the depository table, his vacantly smiling wife stood behind it. Hedges' hooded eyes surveyed the hall and saw the potential trouble. There were not enough girls to go around and the bulk of the female guests were either middle-aged or elderly. Those civilians not dancing with their women watched the luckier soldiers with jealous eyes. And many of the unattached soldiers were clustered in groups, surreptitiously lacing their glasses of punch with stronger liquid from hip flasks.

Hedges unbuckled his saber belt. "You have this," he told the preacher. "I'll keep my side iron."

The preacher blinked. "Everybody else has been most co-operative, Captain," he urged.

"You say a little prayer they keep being that way, reverend," he muttered, and treated the man to a hard stare.

Jeannie gave the preacher a sympathetic smile, then scuttled after Hedges as he made his way around the edge of the dancers towards the food table.

"Can you dance, Joe?" she asked after watching him munch hungrily at a cold beef sandwich.

"I ain't never seen any point in it," he said, surveying the hall again and spotting Forrest and several of the troop openly passing around a whiskey bottle. "Man can't get his arms around a girl any other way, then he's probably the fag he looks tripping around out there."

His face showered scorn on the dancers.

"Then why'd you come?" she asked.

He almost spat on the floor, but held back. "Food's better than the cookhouse gives out, and it's free."

"I didn't think you were a mean man, Joe."

"Most of what I get, I send to my brother," he told her. "He's building up the farm."

Jeannie took a deep breath, preparing to tax Hedges on his plans for after the war and whether she could figure in them. But the sudden movement out on the floor and the raised voice stopped her before she could begin.

"That's my wife you're pawing, soldier!"

The music continued for a few chords, then faded. The dancers fell back, leaving three figures in the center of the floor. One was a large man of middle age who looked like a farmer in his Sunday best. Another was a small, frightened-looking woman about the same age who was holding together the front of her dress where it had been torn. The third was an infantryman who was so drunk he could hardly stand up now that the big man had parted him from the woman. He was young enough to be the woman's son.

"Oh, dear," the preacher's wife said into the sudden silence.

The guilty infantryman grinned stupidly. "I weren't doing nothing," he slurred.

"He touched me!" the woman said shrilly.

"She feel good, Luke?" a voice called.

The infantryman giggled. "All I touched was whalebone," he answered.

"You oughta stayed with it," came the response as the woman's husband launched a haymaker towards the infantryman.

Cries of alarm and yells of anger were suddenly strident in the hall as the soldier took the punch on the point of his chin and reeled backwards, his arms flailing. Hedges reached for his gun and when Jeannie tried to hamper him, he shoved her roughly away, crashing into the food table. Soldiers and civilians turned to face each other and prepared to emulate the violence that had just occurred. Hedges aimed high over the heads of the crowd and squeezed the Colt's trigger. But at the same instant the revolver cracked, a louder report sounded, synchronizing with the shattering of glass and a man's scream of agony.

The soldier was seventeen years old and had a passionate belief in the cause of the Abolitionists. He had come in with the new recruits that afternoon, firmly resolved to fight for the liberty of all who were not oppressors. He died in the process of drinking a fruit punch, the bullet smashing the glass and imbedding splinters over his face then entering the roof of his mouth and gushing out with a spout of blood at the back of his neck.

As Hedges whirled towards the window through which the bullet had entered, a dozen other panes smashed under the impact of bullets which whined into the crowded hall and found their marks on Union soldiers. Hedges got off a shot and dived for the floor as the screams and shouts rose in volume and there was a great rush towards the table loaded with weapons. Civilians and women dropped to the floor and scuttled on all fours towards the hall entrance as more bullets whined over their heads and the Union men grabbed the first gun that came to hand and began to return the fire. Tables and chairs were overturned to provide inadequate cover against the murderous crossfire.

"Damn Yankees!" a man taunted from beyond one of the broken windows.

"You want entertaining?" cried another.

"We'll give you a show!" called a third.

Another fusillade of shots rang out. The infantryman knocked down by the civilian tried to stagger to his feet. One bullet shattered his right knee and another took him in the left elbow. He fell to the floor, writhing and screaming. A third bullet gouged a great furrow across his forehead and as the blood curtained down into his eyes his jugular vein was punctured. A soldier who had been cowering in a corner made a sudden run towards the gun table and began to slide frantically in the spilled blood, arms flailing to keep his balance.

"Slide, man, slide!" a rebel voice yelled in delight.

The soldier began to fall, and was helped on his way by two bullets crashing into the back of his head.

There were perhaps twenty dead in the meeting house, their bodies sprawled in a variety of blood-soaked attitudes. The preacher also looked dead, sitting upright in a corner by the door, one side of his face covered with shiny scarlet. The surviving soldiers were crouched in cover, those who had reached the table firing out the windows, the others trying to make themselves as small as possible.

Hedges could see no women left inside the building and noticed that Jeannie was gone. The shooting from outside seemed to have ceased and in a few moments the trapped men stopped shooting. The silence was suddenly oppressive, menacing in its solidity.

"Hey, Captain?" a voice called.

"What is it, Seward?" Hedges answered.

"This cruddy town off-limits even when the cruddy rebs come in and shoot it up?"

"Just like the goddam cavalry," an embittered infantryman yelled. "Always expect more goddam cavalry to help you out."

"Yeah, don't you know they're always late!"

"Cut out the smart mouth!" Hedges ordered, as hoofbeats sounded outside, then several shots and the high-pitched screams of frightened women.

"They're taking them!" a man yelled. "They're taking the . . ."

His words were cut off by a shot and a wet groan. Hedges came out from behind the table and went at a crouching run across the body-littered floor. When he made it without drawing fire, the others streamed after him, out into the warm, early summer night. Two men lay dead in the dusty street, one of them the man whose wife had been molested. Several elderly women were sitting on the sidewalk or squatting in the street, wringing their hands and weeping. Two men looked with terror into the night which was swallowing up the sound of retreating horses. From the other direction came the din of noisy saloons which had effectively screened the sounds of the raid from the camp, no more than dots of fire and lamp lights in the velvet black of the darkness at the far side of town.

As Hedges looked frantically around for Jeannie, one of the civilians turned to confirm his suspicion.

"They took the women," the man said, tears coursing down his cheeks. "They took my daughter."

Anger was a hard weight in Hedges' stomach. His mouth formed into a snarl and his eyes narrowed to the merest slits. He reached out a rock-steady hand and grasped a bunch of the man's shirt front.

"Who took the woman?" he demanded, his mouth spitting the words as if they were pieces of jagged metal.

"Terry's Raiders," the man spilled from trembling lips. "Bill Terry and his gangsters."

"Army?" Hedges demanded.

He was holding the man's shirt so tightly the civilian was beginning to choke. "They wear uniforms," he croaked.

"How many?"

"Dozen of them, including Terry."

"Eleven of them, Captain," Forrest said from the alley at the side of the building. "One of us got in a lucky shot."

The sergeant emerged from the dark mouth of the alley. Behind him were Rhett and Douglas, supporting between them a young man clad in dishevelled Confederate grey. The prisoner looked dazed and the side of his head was dark with congealed blood from a bullet graze above his right ear. Hedges pushed the civilian away and moved across to stand before the injured raider. The look of cold evil on Hedges' face forced the man to gather his senses.

"I ain't gonna talk," he said in a deep, Southern drawl.

There was absolute silence as Hedges pushed the Colt into its holster, his hands moving in slow, measured movements. Even the women ceased their weeping and looked with bated breath towards the group at the mouth of the alley, gripped by the tension.

"There's a war on," Hedges said softly. "Man can't be that definite about anything."

Suddenly, the action a blur, he reached his right hand up to his neck and brought it down again, the blade of the razor flashing in the meager lighting from the meeting house doorway. The raider drew back against the grip of Rhett and Douglas as the razor slashed within a hair's-breadth of his wan face.

"Close shave," Hedges muttered, and reached out to rest the flat of the blade against the bridge of the raiders' nose. It was quite a large nose.

"Cut him, Captain," Rhett urged with high excitement.

"Shut up," Hedges snarled.

Rhett continued to grin drunkenly as Hedges leaned close to the raider.

"I'm a prisoner of war," the man pleaded.

"You're a hunk of meat on two legs," Hedges corrected. "Where are your pals holed up?"

"I ain't gonna tell you that," the man said, then gave a high-pitched scream.

The razor sliced under the flesh and travelled down to the tip. Blood spouted and a broad strip of skin fell forward and dangled in front of the man's mouth. One of the women fainted and nobody went to her aid for all attention was riveted upon the agonized face of the prisoner.

"I reckon he knows something, Captain," Forrest said with an icy grin.

Seward giggled.

"Been out in the sun too long," Rhett murmured to the prisoner. "You're starting to peel."

"You bastard Yankee!" the prisoner hissed.

"Hard man," Douglas said to Hedges.

"But soft in the head," Hedges replied, prodding forward with the razor and then slashing downwards.

The raider winced, then screamed. What seemed to be a length of red yarn appeared across his right cheek from the corner of the eye to the corner of the mouth. Blood washed down the lower half of his cheek.

"Stop it!" a woman shrieked. "Stop this."

The civilian who had been crying lashed out a fist and the woman crumpled. "They took my daughter," he rasped.

Down the dark street, a piano began to jangle and high-heeled shoes slapped a stage. Men roared their approval of the dancers.

"I can go deeper," Hedges urged his victim. "They took my girl."

The prisoner gathered spittle in his mouth. As he ejected it, Hedges ducked and then came up with the razor flashing. The blade hooked into the corner of the man's mouth and raked upwards. When it came free of the flesh, the lower half of the man's left cheek flapped away. His exposed back teeth ground together in a grin of agony. Blood cascaded down to widen the stain on the front of his uniform. Tears spilled from his dark eyes before he screwed them shut. His mouth moved, but emitted only a gurgle.

"I don't think he can talk, sir," Scott said, a little nervously.

"He just ain't trying," Hedges answered. "Maybe he ain't too worried about his face. Drop his pants."

While Rhett and Douglas continued to keep the

weakened prisoner upright, Forrest moved forward and reached for the raider's belt buckle.

"Now don't get excited, Bob," he murmured to Rhett.

The prisoner sucked in his belly. "Wait," he croaked, spraying blood with the word. "Brookerville. They're at Brookerville."

Hedges gripped Forrest's shoulder and jerked him away. "Where's that?" he demanded.

"Ten miles. East."

"That's right." This from the man whose daughter had been kidnapped. "It's just a village. Hardly that."

"Obliged," Hedges said to the raider and slit his throat. Rhett and Douglas allowed the limp form of the dead man to fold onto the ground in a widening circle of blood.

"My life, you didn't have to kill him," a Jewish voice exclaimed from the shadowed facade of a storefront across the street.

"With a face like that, I did him a favor," Hedges muttered as he stooped to wipe the blood from his razor, using the uniform tunic of the dead man.

"Such favors, don't do me."

Hedges turned to stare levelly into the wan face of one of the musicians who was regarding him with horrified contempt. "You got a big mouth, fiddler."

The words were low, but vibrant with menace. The man backed away, as if the voice had a physical strength which was pushing him into the shadows.

"We goin' after the crud, Captain?" Forrest asked, cutting across the pool of tense silence that engulfed this end of the street.

"What do you think?"

"I think you think a lot of a certain party, sir," the sergeant answered.

"And now is the time for all good men to come to the aid of that party," Rhett said excitedly.

"And we're just the type," Scott said.

"Right," Hedges answered, turning to start along the street.

The others fell in around him, the pace quickening.

"You didn't have to kill him," the fiddler yelled after them when they were almost out of earshot.

"Go jump off a roof!" Seward shrieked back at him.

*　*　*

The Skyline Hotel was in a prime position on the very peak of Nob Hill, offering panoramic views across the city to the bright blue of the ocean in the west and to the darker blue of the ragged mountains in the opposite direction. It was an impressive building of stone and had an entrance flanked by marble pillars. A Negro dressed in red velvet livery took charge of Vic Paxton's horse and, despite himself, the young deputy was more than a little over-awed as he entered the plush lobby with its wall-to-wall carpeting and flimsy-looking furniture.

The people in the lobby were all dressed expensively and the glances they cast in Paxton's direction were designed to make him feel ill at ease in his dusty work clothes. But as he crossed to the polished desk he rubbed his arm across the left side of his chest and swung slightly from side to side to ensure that everybody saw the glint of the tin star. But the people were rich enough to be above the law and failed to be impressed. The woman behind the desk liked Paxton's immature good looks and smiled brightly at him, her blue eyes wide with unashamed interest.

"Good morning, officer," she greeted.

She was about thirty and her youthful prettiness was receding. She attempted to cheat time with a great deal of make-up. Morning sun highlighted the

64

lie. Paxton kept his expression hard as he dug the to-ken from his vest pocket and held it up.

"This one of yours?" he demanded.

The woman fluttered her eyelids, the lashes as false as her youth. "I'm just the receptionist, dearie," she taunted.

"I didn't mean personal," Paxton told her.

"You're rather early. I'm off at midday and you wouldn't need that."

She was dressed in a high-necked gown of green silk, nipped in tight at the waist. The fabric clung close to her upper body and swelled as she sucked in her breath. With an effort, Paxton was able to keep his eyes locked on her face.

"Emmeline Greer?" he asked.

The woman shook her head. "You're too late, feller."

"Why?"

"She's gone."

"Where?" Paxton snapped.

Already aware that she had failed to generate any interest from the young deputy, the woman dropped all attempts to be appealing.

"How the hell would I know? There's plenty of other five-dollar screws upstairs." Her voice was low, inaudible to the others in the lobby, but harsh.

"When did she go?" Paxton demanded.

"This morning, early. Madam don't keep girls here if they don't want to stay."

"She go alone?"

"Guy called for her. In a carriage. Looked like she was going to a ritzy place."

"Why? What makes you think that?"

"It was a high-priced rig. New paint and lots of pol-ish. Had this picture on the doors."

"What picture?" Paxton sensed he was on to a strong lead and the excitement of this was audible in his voice.

"How much it worth to you?" the woman asked, her expression suddenly avaricious.

"Five bucks," Paxton told her.

She nodded, satisfied with the offer. "Kind of Biblical. An apple and a snake."

Paxton grinned and slapped the token down on the desk. "Thanks," he said as he turned.

"What's this?" she demanded.

"It says on it that it's worth five dollars," he pointed out.

"Not to me it's not," she snapped.

Paxton shrugged. "You've just been screwed for five bucks," he said, and strolled back across the lobby, filled with enough confidence to force San Francisco's gentry to turn away from his steady, clear-eyed stare.

As the deputy was retrieving his horse from the elegantly attired Negro high on Nob Hill, the carriage which had taken Emmeline Greer away from the Skyline Hotel was parked outside of the jailhouse in a less well-endowed section of the city. A coachman was polishing the brasswork with a soft cloth. Inside the building, the rig's owner was staring at Edge with an expression of unadulterated hatred that seemed strong enough to melt the iron bars of the cell.

"You killed the only thing in the world that I give a damn about," Lydia Eden said, her voice trembling with emotion.

"No, lady," Edge answered. "Twice."

Her brow furrowed.

Edge picked at his teeth with a fingernail. He talked around his hand. "No, I didn't kill him. That's once. No, because for anyone that gets as rich as you, money is the only thing to give a damn about. That's twice."

"Watch your mouth!" Red Railston snapped.

Edge was stretched out on the rancid mattress, resting his head against the end wall, his black hat crushed up to give a modicum of comfort to the tenderness of his skull. Railston was resting his heavy rump against the corner of his desk. The woman stood on the stone floor in the center of the office, out of reach of the bars. She was in her mid-fifties and once may have been as pretty as her son had been handsome: but some of her long years had been hard ones and had taken their toll. Her face was long and thin enough so that the bone structure showed through and the yellow-tinged, parchment-textured skin seemed to be draped in flaccid creases from her tiny, field-green eyes to the delicate line of her pointed jaw, with her thin mouth as a slightly more pronounced, darker colored fold. Her hair was short cut and the color of autumn wheat stubble. Although her body, concealed from neck to ankle in a deep black dress, was so thin it was almost painful to look at, there was about the woman an aura of strength which emanated from her spiritual, rather than her physical, make-up. Thus, Railston's bulk appeared to shrink into insignificance beside the subtler power of Lydia Eden.

"What you going to do, Red?" Edge taunted. "Hang me for talking out of turn?"

Mint Julep, who had backed into a corner of his cell when Lydia Eden entered, could not suppress a giggle.

"It could happen to you, alky!" Railston roared, turning his anger towards an easier target.

"You'll hang, saddletramp," the woman spat at Edge. "And burn in the fires of hell for eternity."

Edge worked a piece of old meat out from his teeth and spat it towards the bars. It sailed between them and hit the floor close to the hem of the woman's skirt. Railston came away from the desk, his face dark with anger. Lydia Eden raised a bony arm across his chest and it pulled up the marshal as effectively as a levelled Winchester.

"Leave him!" she ordered. "Noon tomorrow will be his time."

"Money buys speed, too," Edge muttered.

"Judge Ryan can't be bought," Railston answered.

"That's right," Mint Julep put in. "He runs a straight court." He turned sad eyes towards Edge. "Course, he always hangs a killer."

"And you killed my little Chad," Lydia Eden accused.

"I didn't kill him," Edge answered softly. "He was so dumb rich he was an accident looking for someplace to happen. Last night he found the right scene."

"He was a fine boy," Lydia Eden retorted, the abhorrence gleaming from deep within her eyes.

Edge held her gaze and the gleam in his eyes was as strong as her hate. But the emotion he showed was of scorn. "Why did you come here, Mrs. Eden?" he asked quietly.

She showed a row of small, very white teeth in a vicious sneer. "The marshal told me you were full of pride. I wanted to see it. Then at noon tomorrow I'll be able to see just how much of a snivelling coward you are when they put the rope around your neck."

The hate from within the woman seemed to chill the air in the sunlit room. Railston grinned through the bars. "Man like him will die hard, Mrs. Eden," he said happily.

"Happens to every man that gets hung," Edge replied easily, continuing to stare into the crinkled face of the woman. "Did you know a man that's hung ejaculates as his neck snaps?"

Lydia Eden sucked in her breath and drew back, shocked.

"You've got a filthy mouth!" Railston bellowed,

reaching for one of his guns but not hooking it from the holster.

"I get it!" Mint Julep yelled, cackling. "I get it. A man dies hard. He's gotta be to do that."

Mrs. Eden glanced at the delighted drunk, wrinkling her nose. Edge grinned at him, enjoying the woman's sudden change from ice-cold hatred to feverish embarrassment. "Shows a man is brave to the end," Edge said to the drunk.

"How's that?" Mint Julep asked, still giggling as Railston's face colored to a deep purple.

"Way he keeps his pecker up," Edge said.

"I get it, I get it," Mint Julep shrieked as Lydia Eden whirled and strode hurriedly to the door.

Fuming, Railston drew his side iron and pumped a bullet into the cell. It smashed into the wall and showered the drunk with stone chips. Mint Julep shrieked and cowered into a ball, hands clasped above his head, knees pressed hard against his chest.

"Hold your stupid tongue," the marshal bellowed. "There's a lady present."

"Not any more," Edge tossed in.

Railston snapped his head around in time to see the hem of Lydia Eden's mourning dress trailing over the threshhold. He scooted after her to help her into the carriage. Edge looked at the trembling form of Mint Julep.

"Didn't we meet someplace before?" he asked.

Mint Julep's eyes had been screwed shut. Now he opened one and breathed a sigh of relief as he saw the office was empty. He opened the other eye and gave Edge a watery stare, his face contorting into a thoughtful frown. After a few moments he shook his head.

"I don't know, mister. Sure as hell you never bought me no drink. I always remember guys who bought me a drink."

He began to pick pieces of stone from his clothing as Edge wriggled down to spread his body full length on the mattress, then covered his face with the crumpled hat. His mind peered backwards through the curtains of time past.

CHAPTER FIVE

The preacher's wife had been sick. The vomit had spewed from her slack mouth and formed into a hard, crusted trail over her chin, down her neck and across the limp, sac-like elongations that were her aging breasts. Her naked body was bowed backwards over the bar in the Brookerville Saloon, with her ankles hooked under the brass rail and her arms extended high above her head, held rigid by ropes tied to her wrists and hitched to the self behind the bar. She had emptied her stomach as the man entered her and fainted before he was finished. Two other women approaching middle years were dead, both as naked as the preacher's wife. One hung upside-down by her ankles from a ceiling beam, dripping blood which oozed out of two large bullet holes in her stomach. The other had been crucified upon the top of an upended table leaning against a wall, suffering long minutes of agony from the nails driven through her flesh before a merciful bayonet had been driven deep into her stomach and twisted viciously to bring death.

Four younger women, among them Jeannie Fisher, crouched against the wall, trying to hide their nakedness with their hands as two of Terry's Raiders menaced them with Springfield rifles. On the far side of the bar-room, the remainder of the guerillas lounged arrogantly around two tables, firing their imagination with whiskey straight from stolen bottles as they waited for their leader to command further entertainment. In an army only now, after long years of war, beginning to understand the need for discipline, the Confederate raider groups were becoming an anachronism. Bands such as that commanded by Bill Terry were comprised of outlaws and gunslingers who regarded the war as an opportunity to legalize their bestial brutality. They recognized no rules except those laid down by the strongest member of the group and even such strength could be undermined or merely ignored should a leader show signs of giving the war effort precedence over the less ambitious aims of his men.

But Terry would never fall into such an untenable position because he wore the Confederate grey with the same intention of his men—to kill, rape and loot with an impunity that only a Union bullet could penetrate. Thus he had organized and led the raid on Murfreesboro with no tactical objective in mind except to alleviate the boredom of himself and his men after a long period of inactivity.

Terry was a self-appointed captain who had long ago ceased to demand the privileges of rank beyond those he was able to maintain by his speed and accuracy with a captured Union officer's saber. He was not a big man, but he was built with a solid compactness which, allied with his agility, more than compensated for what he lacked in brute strength. He was forty years old and had learned the art of cruelty as slavemaster on a Virginia cotton plantation before joining up with an ex-safemaker who decided it was more profitable to blow open strongboxes than to build them. The nucleus of the raiders was formed in the year before the Civil War exploded into being, and each man had greeted the opening of hostilities with gleeful delight. And the bloody trail they had cut across the intervening years served only to heighten their anticipation for newer, more depraved experiences. So that, in the sputtering lamplight of the Brookerville Saloon, surrounded by the empty buildings of a deserted village, the men of Terry's Raiders revelled in the sight of the women's naked dead bodies and waited with slavering, whiskey-run lips for the black-bearded man with a captain's insignia to call forward the next terrified victim.

His dark eyes red veined from the liquor, Terry slapped down his bottle on the table and swished his saber around to point at a fresh-faced youngster who had been drinking without enthusiasm and whose meanness of features was underplayed by a deep anxiety.

"I reckon the Yankees killed your twin, Matt," Terry said coldly. "Or if they did not, he'll be wishing they had right now. You take the little girl with the birthmark on her ass. You take out your revenge on her, Matt."

The youngster hesitated for only a moment, then stood up, swaying slightly with the effects of the whiskey. The others roared out a cheer, then fell silent as Matt walked with slow care across the space cleared in the center of the bar-room.

"You're the one," he said, halting close to the dangling body of the upended woman and pointing a wavering hand between the two guards to where a young blonde girl of eighteen was crouched.

The girl whimpered and pressed herself against the rough wood of the wall. One of the guards, who had first crucified and then disembowelled the woman given to him, jabbed the muzzle of his rifle into the

72

girl's narrow hip. The second guard, who had bound and raped the preacher's wife, reached down, grasped the girl's left breast and jerked her away from the wall, flinging her to the feet of Matt.

"No!" she screamed, scrambling onto her knees and clasping her hands together, looking up at the young man with her eyes imploring him to be merciful.

"You're a Southern woman!" Terry bellowed, slamming his fist against the table and knocking over a bottle. "And you were dancing with Yankee crud. What do you say, men?"

"Guilty!" they chorused.

"Please," the girl pleaded in a whisper, her eyes and those of Matt locked on a stare that seemed to set them apart from everybody else in the room.

Matt felt a stirring in his loins, as he tore his gaze away from the girl's face and drank in her naked paleness.

"Slip it to her good Matthew!" one of the raiders urged. "But save a piece for me."

"Yeah," agreed another. "Can't afford to let the young stuff go to waste."

"Please," the girl whispered again, unclasping her hands and reaching up to grip the hem of Matt's tunic.

He looked into her face again and suddenly his own features clouded, the lust dying. Hope rose within the girl, but it was fleeting. Matt saw the familiar face of his brother superimposed upon the girl's youthful prettiness and his mind was abruptly blazing with fury that he was now without kin in the world: for he knew that Theo had to be dead. Hatred turned his face to stone as he drew the .44 Remington from its holster.

"What a goddam waste," one of the men said bitterly, raising a bottle to console himself with whiskey.

Terry snarled, levered himself up out of his chair

73

and slashed out with the saber. The edge of the blade smashed into the bottle, shattering the glass. Spilled liquor cascaded down the man's front. "I gave the woman to him!" Terry thundered. "He does as he chooses."

The man seemed on the point of snapping a retort, but one look into Terry's eyes, glinting along the blade of the sword, drove him into mumbling subservience. "Sure, Bill," he muttered.

The girl suddenly screamed and staggered to her feet, turning her back upon her executioner as she made a run for the door. Matt crooked his arm and rested the barrel of the revolver across it, sighting carefully along the length of black metal. The girl screamed again as she pitched forward, gushing blood from the back of her left knee. As she writhed in agony, she rolled over on to her back. Matt carefully altered his aim and sent his second bullet into the front of the girl's right leg. More blood, mixed with splinters of her kneecap, sprayed across the wooden floor.

"Yankees' whore!" Terry bellowed in recrimination.

The girl's agony and terror were now voiced as a continuous wail. Two quick shots smashed her elbows and her own blood greased the boards as she swung over on to her stomach and endeavored to snake her body towards the bat-swing doors. With infinite slowness, Matt moved forward, and just as the girl's head began to push under one of the doors, he lifted a foot and brought it down hard, grinding the heel of his boot into her back. Her wail was choked off by a gasping sob. Only able to move her head, she screwed it round and looked up at him with eyes made dull by agony.

"What's your name, girl?" he asked, splitting the pregnant silence that had descended upon the room as the raiders waited expectantly for her death.

"Peggy Sue," she rasped. "Why?"

He shrugged and then aimed the Remington. "No reason. I guess it really doesn't matter any more." He squeezed the trigger and the bullet tore a ragged hole in the side of her head. He turned to face the men around the tables, some of whom were sneering at him for the pleasure they had been denied by his action in killing the girl.

"You made it easy for her," Terry accused. It was he who had strung up the woman from the beam and used the glowing end of a cigar to burn target marks on her stomach before spinning her and sending two fast bullets to obliterate the signs of his torture. "Dave, the Captain's whore is yours."

As the trembling Jeannie was prodded out towards the center of the saloon, a barrel-chested man with a harelip moved towards her, his mouth drooling in anticipation of what was to come.

"Careful you don't split your pants," a raider yelled to a gust of laughter as the thick-set man gave visible sign of his arousal.

Matt, his thirst for revenge satisfied, glanced regretfully down at the blood-soaked, still form of the girl named Peggy Sue, then fastened his attention on Jeannie's slim nakedness, trembling before Dave's powerful figure. Another expectant silence fell like an invisible blanket over the saloon as Dave reached out a dirt-ingrained, enormous hand towards one of the soft, tremulous mounds of the girl's breasts.

The two shots sounded in unison, drowning out the smash of glass. The bullet from Forrest's Henry took Matt in the back of the head and flipped him forward into a death roll. Hedges' shot, fired through a window, drilled a neat hole through the center of Dave's sweating palm and buried itself into the unresponsive flesh of the hanging woman. There was no blood. She had been dead too long. The sound of breaking glass

75

was abruptly loud as other windows were smashed and a dozen rifle muzzles bristled into the room.

"All good things have got to end!" Rhett called.

Most of the rebel raiders were too drunk from hard liquor, blood and lust to consider the wisdom of discretion in the situation. And as they snatched for their weapons and dived to the floor in search of cover, the more circumspect could do nothing but follow the lead set.

"Move it, Jeannie!" Hedges shouted as the rebels got off their first shots and the Union troopers answered with a volley.

The girl seemed rooted to the spot, but as the head of Dave suddenly exploded under the impact of three heavy caliber bullets, she leapt towards the bar and over it, feeling the warm blood of the dead man running down her face. As the bullets crisscrossed the saloon, it was like the meeting house at Murfreesboro again, but with the roles of the Union and Confederate soldiers reversed. This time it was the men in blue who had the solid cover of stout walls while the rebels were forced to flatten themselves against the floor or scamper behind overturned tables and chairs in an effort to seek refuge from the hail of angry bullets.

A rebel crouching behind a chair died with a scream as a bullet tore into his back. He pitched forward, knocking aside a table shielding another rebel. Exposed, the second man tried to run to the bar, but suddenly began to stagger about blindly as a bullet smashed into a bottle and sprayed splinters of glass into his face, blinding him and splitting open one cheek. He crashed headfirst out through a window, where Billy Seward was waiting having just reloaded his rifle.

"Nice of you to drop by," Seward said with a snigger as he ground the muzzle of the Henry into the man's lacerated cheek and squeezed the trigger.

76

Another of Terry's Raiders successfully worked his way around to the door of the saloon, snaking along in the angle of the wall and the floor. As he poked his head under the bat-swings and looked wide-eyed along the street, Forrest brought a boot down hard on the man's neck. He rested the rifle muzzle against the rebel's ear.

"If you gotta go, you gotta go," the Union sergeant intoned in mocking regret. "So long, reb."

He squeezed the trigger and the man's brains spattered on the sidewalk.

Alternately peering through the window and ducking back out of sight, Hedges kept up a regular rate of fire into the saloon. Most of the troopers adopted the same tactic and few rebels survived the initial assault. But those who did were able to use the heavy pall of acrid gunsmoke as a screen to scuttle into more substantial cover. The smoke was like a swirling mist within the saloon and the troopers' firing became sporadic, then trailed off.

"I think we killed all the bastards," Roger Bell yelled after long seconds during which no sound was heard.

But then a dozen pair of ears picked up a faint scratching on one side of the saloon and as a whimper spilled from a dry throat, six rifles cracked. The two naked girls, who had curled themselves into quivering balls during the height of the gunfight, screamed and splashed their blood across the wall and floor. Two rebels fired at the same gun flash and a Union trooper leaped back from a window, crimson fountains spurting from the pulp of his eye sockets. Ten troopers sent a volley of shots towards the rebels, positioned behind an upright piano with no front. The bullets jangled among the strings and crashed through the wood at the back. One man died at once, his chest peppered with blossoming holes. The second man ran into the open, pouring blood from a wound in his

77

groin. A trooper saw his target as a mere flitting shadow and leaned in through the window for a better shot. Terry, who was crouching down behind the solid cover of the end of the bar, raised his saber and lashed out with it. The trooper folded his body over the window ledge, his head hanging awkwardly, attached to his shoulders by a few slimy red tendons. A half-dozen bullets from other guns ended the screaming, ungainly run of the rebel who had been wounded.

Terry heard a sound at the far end of the bar and moved into a shadowed area, leaving behind him an untidy pile of dead raiders, hopeful of finding some survivors.

"May God have mercy on your soul," a woman's voice said weakly.

Terry threw himself back against the storage cupboards behind the bar and looked up, his bearded face becoming a mask of shock and fear. But then he forced a cold grin. Incredibly, the preacher's wife was untouched by the barrage of bullets that had whined across the saloon and now she was looking down at the leader of the raiders, her head inverted between her outstretched arms.

"I thank you for the thought, ma'am," Terry said, raising himself slightly, then thrusting upwards with a powerful jerk of his arm.

The woman's body arched under the force of the stabbing blow and then became limp against the pull of the ropes. The saber had entered between her shoulder blades at an acute angle, the point finding her heart. Her blood gushed on to Terry's hand as he withdrew the weapon and continued on down the bar in a half-crouch, his boots crunching on glass shards from broken bottles.

The troopers heard the sounds of his progress and a hail of bullets were showered towards him, burying themselves in the stout wood of the bar or shattering more bottles to rain glass and liquor down upon him.

"Why, you're better than my best man," Terry murmured when he reached the end of the bar and found who had made the noise that had attracted him.

Instead of one of his raiders, he saw the pale, naked form of Jeannie Fisher. The girl was hunched into a knee-hugging posture behind the metal sink used for washing glasses. Fear had drained her of color and the only relief against the whiteness of her flesh was the drying splashes of Dave's blood. Terror had also exhausted her will to resist and she could emit only a meek gasp as the raider's arm encircled her, the hand fastening on her breast. And then a choked sob when the sticky blade of the saber was rested against her throat, forcing up the chin.

"Hey, Yankees!" Terry bellowed.

Two more shots rang out and the bullets thudded into a wooden barrel.

"Hold it!" Hedges yelled.

"Who's the boss out there?" Terry wanted to know.

"I am," Hedges answered, beginning to reload the Henry.

"We need to make a deal."

Hedges worked the action to pump a shell into the breech. All around the saloon the slap of metal against metal told of more reloading.

"Keep talking," Hedges called. He was crouched down, below and to the side of the window, suspicious of a trap.

"You come for us or the women?"

There was a sound behind Hedges and he whirled, the rifle muzzle lifting.

"Jumpy," Forrest whispered, grinning through the silvered night.

Hedges' eyes glinted. "Stupid," he hissed, and turned

to direct his voice through the window. "How many left?"

"Tell him, ma'am," Terry demanded of the girl, loud enough for the troopers to hear.

When she didn't comply at once, Terry dug his filthy nails into the flesh of her breast. Her voice was pained. "Just me, Joe!"

"Sure a lucky war for you, Captain," Forrest muttered.

Terry laughed. "That your captain out there, ma'am?" he asked rhetorically. "Captain, we really do need to deal."

"Say your piece," Hedges answered, his voice brittle with impotent anger.

"Your girl and me," Terry called. "We're all that's left in here."

"Bill!" A weak voice called from one side of a small dias. "It's Frank. I'm losing blood from my guts."

"Tough," Terry replied. "You can have him, Captain."

"I've already got a man with no guts," Hedges said coldly.

"Sue him, Rhett," Hal Douglas exploded with a snigger.

"I'm leaving with your girl, Captain," Terry snarled, suddenly dropping all pretense at lightness. "I've got a blade holding up her chin and she hasn't got anything on except her birthday suit. And you haven't got a chance of dropping me before I slit her pretty throat."

Terry showed his confidence by straightening up, forcing Jeannie to stand in front of him, shielding him. Although the smell of detonated powder was still thick in the air, mingling with the unmistakable odor of sudden death, the grey smoke was clearing, wafted out of the saloon through the smashed windows.

"Bill!" the wounded man pleaded.

"Just die quietly, Frank," Terry snarled, his evil eyes roving around the windows, seeing the faces of the troopers peering in at him and the girl through the jagged surrounds of smashed glass.

"Any man gets trigger-happy, he'll answer to me." Hedges' warning was a rasp across the silence as Terry forced the girl out from behind the bar.

"Joe," Jeannie murmured. Her eyes rolled and her body, fragilely slim and defenceless in its nakedness against the determined stance of her captor, seemed about to go limp. But the nails dug deeper into her flesh and the saber blade pressed harder against her chin. The pain and the threat revived her.

"I need a horse," Terry said.

"Get him one, Scott," Hedges ordered.

Despite the sprawled bodies and drying blood that formed the background, the central image of the girl in the grip of her tormentor presented an erotic, dreamlike quality and Hedges was perhaps the only Union trooper unaffected by the sight. The Captain had to bark the command again before Scott was able to tear himself away from the window.

"I'm riding out of Brookerville," Terry said evenly as he took slow steps, urging Jeannie ahead of him to the door. "With the girl for two miles. If I don't hear you guys trailing me, I'll turn her loose. If I do hear anything I don't like, I'll cut her loose. You know what I mean?"

"You believe him, sir?" Seward called from the far side of the saloon.

"You want to try a shot at him?" Hedges snarled as Terry and his human shield reached the swing doors.

"Don't do me any favors," Seward called, impersonating the voice of the Jewish fiddler.

As the raider emerged out on to the sidewalk the troopers left their positions and gathered on the street, flanking the saloon entrance. Scott hurried forward with a horse.

"All of you back off," Terry ordered. "And leave your guns where you're standing."

Hedges was the first to comply, dropping his rifle to the rutted ground and sidestepping away several yards. He avoided looking into the imploring eyes of Jeannie, concentrating upon the face of the bearded man. The other troopers followed his example with their guns, but their attention was riveted upon the curves and shaded areas of the girl's body.

"Don't leave me, Bill," the wounded man called from within the saloon, his voice weakening, the fear inside him pitching his tone high.

"Frank always did talk a lot," Terry said and suddenly lifted the girl and cartwheeled her across the neck of the horse, pinning her there with a hand in the small of her back as he switched the position of the saber so that the point was touching the side of her neck. It took little effort for him to swing from the high sidewalk into the saddle of the horse.

For several moments, his back was towards Hedges, and the cavalry captain began to move a hand towards his holstered Colt. But then he stayed it, the decision made in the last fragment of his mind that had not given way to the dehumanizing demands of the war. His orders had come from Rosecrans himself—bring back the women if possible, but wipe out the guerillas at all costs. Now, as he watched the raider heel the horse into a gentle walk, Hedges knew he was making a mistake: that the chances of Jeannie surviving were so long they were incalculable. But he had to disobey the general's orders and give Jeannie her chance—and not from any altruistic motive. For while the girl lived, Hedges could still consider himself a complete man because it was his feeling for her that fed the tiny flame of idealism in his mind. If she died, so would the last shred of human emotion be extinguished and the instincts of the animal would triumph. One day, perhaps, Jamie and the familiar surroundings of the Iowa farm could rekindle the ashes of dead responses, but here in this village of the dead, memories of the past and hopes for the future were so remote they were in another world.

Terry didn't look back as he urged his mount into a faster pace, at first cantering and then galloping, clear of the cluster of buildings and into a small wood through which the trail disappeared.

"Bill!" the wounded man wailed into the silence that descended after the sound of hoofbeats had diminished into the nothingness of distance.

"We goin' after him, sir?" a trooper asked nervously, apprehensive of the impassiveness spread across Hedges' moonlit face.

"Bill!"

"That reb's beginning to bother me, Sergeant," Hedges muttered. "Keep it quiet. We don't want to panic anybody."

A harsh grin of anticipation wreathed Forrest's dirt-streaked face as he went forward and picked up his rifle.

"Get your arms and mount up," Hedges told the troopers as Forrest pushed open the saloon doors and stepped across the bodies of the raider he had killed and the naked girl who had died at Matt's hand.

The wounded raider near the dais was on his side, his splayed hands drenched with blood as he tried to staunch the flow from two bullet holes in his stomach. His eyes were wide, an odd mixture of resignation and fear visible behind the pain.

"Bill went, huh?" he croaked.

Forrest checked there was no gun within reach of the raider, and rested his own rifle against the inverted, bullet-riddled body of the hanging woman, wedging the muzzle between her breasts. He nodded as he approached the man, a hand delving beneath his tunic and coming out with a knife. "Some guys have all the luck, don't they?" he said easily.

Frank's grizzled throat moved in a dry swallow as Forrest crouched beside him.

"He got the girl and you're paying the price, reb. Got any last requests?"

"I'd like a cigarette."

"You smoked too many already," Forrest said with a shake of his head. "They've took years off your life."

He lashed out with the knife and Frank died with a strangled cry as the skin of his throat snapped back to erupt a river of blood from his jugular vein.

"You giving him the last rites in there?" Hedges shouted from outside the saloon.

Forrest retrieved his rifle, cast a final dispassionate look over the carnage around him and pushed through the doors. On the street the troopers were mounted and Seward was holding three spare horses.

"Seems we lost two men," Forrest said as he swung up into the saddle of his mount. "Turn their nags free, Captain?"

Hedges looked hard into the flat eyes of the sergeant and saw they backed up the inference of his words. "Just one," he said with emphasis.

Forrest shrugged as Seward slapped the rump of a spare horse, to send it galloping away down the short street. "That leaves us with one too many," he muttered.

The rest of the troopers sat tense in their saddles, awaiting Hedges' response to Forrest's attempt to rile him.

"It matches the count on big mouths," Hedges hissed as he heeled his mount forward. "Keep it closed until I tell you to open it."

Forrest's face darkened with fury and had the two

of them been alone, Hedges would not have turned his back on the sergeant. But there were too many witnesses and not all of them had more respect for Forrest's iron will than Hedges' rank. So the troop moved off without an explosion of violence, at a slow, quiet pace set by the officer in the lead.

Brookerville became quiet again, looking innocently peaceful in the soft moonglow, with the lights from the saloon windows shining out like welcoming beacons into the night. Not until the warmth of a new day came would the dead begin to give off their bittersweet odor to warn a passing stranger of the horror to which the village was playing host.

The troopers emerged from the far side of the stand of timber and started up a gentle slope towards another clump of trees at the crest. The trail was baked hard and showed no sign of the passage of a horse, but to each side the terrain was a featureless tract of virgin countryside which would have revealed Terry's plan had he chosen to veer to left or right. The horse soldiers rode in a single file column, with Hedges at the head and Forrest bringing up the rear, leading the spare mount. Nobody spoke and even the horses seemed to understand the necessity for stealth so that their occasional snorts were almost apologetic.

"Light ahead, sir," Douglas whispered from immediately behind Hedges as they reached the halfway point of the slope.

"And it ain't no sun coming up," Hedges muttered. "Let's move it."

He dug his heels hard into the flanks of his horse to send it racing ahead and the troopers were quick to follow, streaming up the incline towards the unmistakable glow of firelight that was starkly outlining the trees in the center of the clump. As Hedges swung off the trail, plunging towards the brightness of the fire, he heard a terrifying scream and his face became

85

contorted by a mask of hate-filled fury as he realized his gamble had failed.

He burst clear of the trees into a glade just as a second scream cut through the crackling of burning brush. His horse tried to stop too suddenly in compliance with the hard-pulled reins and went into a sideways roll. Hedges kicked free of the stirrups and snatched the rifle from its boot as he leapt clear. He landed on his shoulder and turned over twice before a tree trunk halted him, jarring every bone in his body. Rage was a red mist in front of his hooded eyes and he looked through it at the yellow flames which were dancing convulsively around the foot of a towering elm. The burning brush gave off a dry, clean smell, but suddenly this was swamped by the evil odor of charring flesh.

Jeannie Fisher's body, held tight against the tree trunk by lariat rope, was no longer pale. The lower half was completely enveloped in the writhing flames which, even as Hedges stared, rose higher and blackened her flesh with each wicked lick. As the troopers broke into the clearing and slid from their horses to gape in horrified silence, a stray spark rose and started a fresh fire in the girl's hair, dribbling flames down her face. She was already dead, but Hedges moved without a consideration for the fact, dragging himself to his feet and stumbling towards the crude pyre. But even as the flames leapt higher, generating the heat to drive him back, the restraining ropes burned through Jeannie's body, no longer recognizable as having human form, toppled forward into the seat of the fire.

"Like I said," Forrest muttered to a trooper standing beside him. "One too many."

The trooper looked at the sergeant with unconcealed contempt but then, as the fire found new moisture in the woman's body and hissed it into

cloying vapor, the man's face drained of color and
he folded his body forward, vomiting forth his reaction to the horror. Two other men emptied their stom-
achs in similar fashion. Others turned away, steeling
themselves against the effects of shock. Only two men
watched the fire until the last visible remains of Jeannie Fisher had been consumed by the flames. Hedges
stared with mounting rage, the fury blazing in his
eyes and reaching a strength that matched that of the
fire itself. But every man has an emotional limit and,
when the captain gained his, a transformation over-
came him. Within him, that final sliver of humanity
ceased to exist. Outwardly, his expression melted and
then solidified into a new line. He turned slightly, to
look at Forrest: and there was no longer a red mist to
cloud his vision. The eyes of the two men examined
each other's faces in minute detail over the period of
a split second and then met, peering into the mind of
the other.

"Welcome to the club, Captain," Forrest said.

Even those men weakened by nausea found themselves compelled to look up at the sergeant and the
captain, for each bystander in the firelit clearing
sensed he was witnessing the near unique event of a
full-grown man being reborn.

"Not yours, Forrest," Hedges answered.

The sergeant shrugged. "It's the same one," he murmured. "You just used a different entrance."

Hedges lifted the Henry and levelled it at Forrest.
The sergeant had left his rifle in the saddle boot and
his holster was buttoned down. "If I was with you,
Forrest," Hedges said evenly, "I'd blast you now, just
because I think you came from the same spawn as the
man who burned my girl. But I need a stronger reason than that."

Forrest was not convinced that Hedges was speaking the truth. He backed off a pace, licking his lips,

forcing his eyes to stop from blinking. "The longer we wait here, the further he'll be away," he said suddenly, quickly.

Hedges allowed the rifle barrel to drop and several troopers gave noisy exit to their pent-up breath. "My problem," the captain said. "Take the men back to Murfreesboro."

"The hell with that!" Seward exclaimed. "I don't figure to spend any more time sitting on my ass and doin' drill in no camp."

Hedges spun towards him, the rifle snapping into a firing position again. With the fire blazing behind him, Hedges sent a dozen enormous shadows across the troopers. "So you figure to die right here?" he snapped.

Seward hung his head under Hedges' steely stare. "You can't do that, Captain," he said.

Hedges drew a bead on Seward's heart.

"We're in a battle situation," Douglas said hurriedly. "He can do it." He looked at Forrest. "Let's go, Frank."

"Ain't nobody gonna go no place."

The voice came from the darkness among the trees and every trooper whirled to look in that direction. But before they could focus on the speaker a host of grey-uniformed figures stepped out of the shadows into the circle of light, muskets aimed. The Union troopers looked one way and then the other, along a solid line of Confederate cavalrymen who faced them from around three sides of the clearing.

"Jesus!" Rhett quavered as he shot his hands into the air. "There must be a hundred of them."

Hedges let his rifle fall to the ground as the rebel detachment parted to allow a man with general's insignia to pass through. "We got here firstest," Hedges said with a sigh. "But they sure got the mostest."

The general swaggered across the clearing and halted in front of Hedges, a look of interest enlivening a slight smile which played at the corners of his mouth. "Hell, Captain," he roared. "I like that. I really like that. I'll have to see if I can't use it sometime. General Nathan Bedford Forrest at your service, sir."

"Any relation, Frank?" Seward called to the sergeant.

Forrest spat into the fire. "Wish he was, Billy," he said bitterly. "Maybe I'd live longer."

His namesake swung towards him, bristling with righteous indignation. "You're lucky, soldier," he bellowed. "You've been captured by honorable men— the cavalry of the Confederate army treats its enemy with respect. You will now surrender your sidearms and all other weapons to my men."

"What do you say, Captain?" Seward called as the line of soldiers advanced and formed a complete circle around the Union troopers. "We gonna let them take us?"

The ring of rebels closed in tighter and Hedges glared at Seward with ill-humor. "No, we ain't," Hedges said flatly. "We're going to dig a hole in the ground and drop into it. Then we're going to empty our side irons at them. When we're out of ammunition we're going to take their muskets and beat them over the head. After that we'll bite the rest to death. Then we'll bury them in the hole, steal their horses and ride into Richmond to blast Jefferson Davis."

Seward was not the only Union trooper who listened in all seriousness to Hedges' monologue and showed surprise when he realized there was a musket pressing against his back.

"Take off your gunbelts," a rebel lieutenant ordered.

"Hell," Hedges muttered for all to hear. "They were too fast for us."

General Forrest was pacing up and down outside the ring of captors. "Firstest with the mostest," he intoned. "First with the most. Yes, sir. I really like that. Kind of line that could make a man famous."

The rebels began to line up their prisoners in marching order.

* * *

Lydia Eden's husband had made his fortune from gold as a Forty-Niner and, largely as a result of his wife's good advice, invested the money in land and cattle. He died young and rich, deeply mourned by an attractive widow who chose to channel her great capacity for love in two directions. Nobody was quite sure whether the unselfish affection she lavished upon her son or the dedication with which she sought to swell her wealth had the more powerful motive. But in material terms, the latter had proved the more rewarding.

The ranch she had called the Garden of Eden was spread over many miles of prime oceanside country, stocked with several thousand head of cattle. Citrus trees grew in patterned rows in well-kept orchards, and maize and wheat fields squared the landscape. At the center of this vast expanse of bountiful land was the big house. Two storys high, with Spanish-style arched windows, it was built of native stone, painted white so that it gleamed in the California sun. Around the main structure were spread the outbuildings, housing the servants and the purebred riding horses, the ornate carriages and the high-priced furnishings which the owner had bought on impulse and found no room for.

Paxton approached the house from the west, aware there was less risk of being seen by the Mexican hands and American overseers employed by Lydia Eden. For while most of the property was under cattle or crops, a wide swathe of rugged, pine-clad terrain sweeping down from the house to the beach had been left untouched to provide the owner with a panoramic view of natural beauty which she regarded as a monument to her late husband. His body was, in fact, buried beneath the simple marker of a solid gold cross among a stand of pine in the center of the vista.

Paxton passed the grave without pausing and made his way along a tree-lined bridle path. It was almost noon and he was sweating with the exertion of walking up the rising ground. His horse he had left on the edge of the beach, grazing on lush grass out of range of salt spray from the surf. The deputy moved cautiously, well aware of the meaning of the signs which had been erected around the perimeter of the property, warning trespassers of the severest penalty for their deeds. Three men had been shot for straying through the fences in pursuit of jackrabbits. Two of them had died.

As he neared the crest of the rise, where the ground flattened out, Paxton veered to the side and then swung around so that he could approach the house from the rear. There was no sign of movement anywhere and even the shade trees were so still they seemed to be made of stone. But there were sounds to disturb the hot, quiet air: the rattle of crocks and cutlery from the house kitchen, the snorting of horses from the stables, the strangely beautiful voice of a Mexican woman singing softly in the servants' quarters.

He waited for more than a minute in the deep shadow of the coachhouse wall, gathering the courage to cross the bright, empty yard which separated him from the dazzling whiteness of the house wall. Then, just as he was about to step into the open, a door swung wide and out of the dimness stepped the slight form of Lydia Eden and the bulky figure of Red Railston. Paxton caught his breath and drew back. Their voices reached him crystal clear through the unmoving blanket of heat.

"I'm relying on you, marshal," Lydia Eden said earnestly. "Every member of the jury must be in no doubt."

Railston smiled as he twisted his hat between his meaty hands. "He'll hang, ma'am. With the gun evidence I'll give and Heffner's testimony to back it, I don't reckon there's any need to grease the jury."

Despite her heavy mourning clothes, Lydia Eden looked as cool as the blue Pacific. Her tone was several degrees lower. "I'm relying on nothing. You do as I say."

Railston bobbed his red head, the gesture almost a bow. "Surely, ma'am. Is the woman still being awkward?"

Mrs. Eden's mouth twitched and then pulled into a straight, tight line. "She won't be in court. I will not have my son's name linked with that of a whore."

"You got her someplace safe?"

"At the beachhouse. She won't be set free until that man is swinging at the end of a rope."

Railston released his hat with one hand and caressed the shiny butt of the Colt riding at his right thigh. "Might be best to keep her quiet for all time, Mrs. Eden," he said pointedly.

The woman's eyes poured scorn on the lawman. "I pay you well to do my bidding, marshal," she said coldly. "If I needed a man to do my thinking, it would *not* be you."

Paxton could not suppress a grin as he saw sudden anger flare in Railston's face, to be immediately transformed into subservience as the woman's rock-hard eyes turned to him.

"Yes, ma'am," the marshal said, bobbing his head again. He put on his hat. "I'll see you in court?"

"That you will," Lydia Eden said and turned, her

skirts swishing, to go back into the house. The door slammed shut behind her. Paxton flattened his body against the hot stone of the wall as Railston strode angrily across the yard.

"Hey, Mex!" the marshal bellowed. "Get my horse out here, pronto."

Paxton chanced a look around the angle of the coachhouse and saw a young peon emerge from the stable, leading Railston's big black stallion. The youngster looked frightened as the lawman scrutinized the animal.

"What's that!" Railston yelled, pointing to a slight discoloration on a brass ring of the bridle.

"It will not come off, senor," the peon said, quaking.

Railston's anger at having to submit to Lydia Eden's insults exploded into a powerful roundhouse punch that caught the peon on the side of the head and sent him crumpling to the dust of the yard.

"It's about siesta time, I guess," the marshal said as he swung up into the saddle and spat down on to the unmoving form of the unconscious youngster.

"Your time will come," Paxton murmured as he watched Railston ride out of the yard. Then he waited until the dust from the horse's hooves had settled before moving away himself, wondering at which point on the property's oceanside frontage he would find the beachhouse. But wherever it was, he would find it and his determination grew stronger every step of the way back to where he had left his horse.

CHAPTER SIX

The boxcar stank with the sweat and fear and the more pronounced odor of men who had been in close, unrelieved confinement for too long. It was one of ten cars strung behind a struggling locomotive racketing through the green fields of rebel-held Georgia. Each had seemed to be filled to capacity with Union prisoners when General Forrest's cavalry troop had halted the train in the early hours of the morning. But under the menace of the guards' muskets, the captives in the first car behind the locomotive had been persuaded to surrender their limited ration of spare space to make room for Hedges and his men. The search for Terry's Raiders, followed by the march to the railroad had taken up the greater part of the night and the new prisoners were able to regard the initial hours of their journey as something of a minor luxury. Wedged between the reluctant press of bodies, sleep came easily to them, their fatigued minds creating a lullaby from the clack of wheels against track. But as the greyness of dawn gave way to the brighter color of a day lit by fierce sunlight, the physical discomfort of the cramped, rancid conditions of their travel gained prominence over the need for rest.

"I think the rebs have won," Scott pronounced as he tried to stretch his legs, and drew a curse from a man whose head he kicked. "They got the whole Union Army packed on this train."

"Yeah," somebody called from the other end of the car. "I hear they got Lincoln firing the boiler."

Hedges, Forrest and Rhett were sitting together, pressed up against the sliding door on one side of the car, forced to keep their legs folded up to their chests by the crush of the other prisoners. But they gained some relief from a steady draught streaming in through a crack where the door did not meet flush with its frame.

"We just gonna sit here, Captain?" Forrest asked irritably after many minutes of silence had passed since their waking.

"What you want to do?" Hedges asked. "Dance with Rhett?"

"You got no call to . . ." Rhett whined.

"No offence, Bob," Forrest cut in. "But you smell bad."

Rhett shrugged. "Nobody told me they didn't have a john on the train."

"You disgust me," Forrest snarled.

"I got a weak bladder," Rhett countered.

"It matches your damn head," Forrest snapped.

"Anyone here got a knife?" Hedges called, raising his voice to be heard above the clatter of the wheels and creaking of the car.

"Yeah," a voice called back, heavy with sarcasm. "The rebs let me keep it. I got a carbine and a couple of pistols as well. What you want to do, Captain? Cut your throat or blow your brains out."

The car was suddenly filled with bitter laughter. Forrest grinned at Hedges. "Seems nobody gives a damn for those bars any more," he said.

The cramped conditions made Hedges' movements slow as he reached a hand behind his neck and drew the razor. The sight of the blade, shining in the shaft of sunlight from the cracked door, wiped the cold humor from the sergeant's face.

Hedges' lips curled back in a grin of his own. "Not now, Forrest," he hissed. "I told you. There has to be a reason. Shove up."

He ground his hip against that of Forrest and a series of groans travelled around the car as one man's need to change position involved every prisoner in shifting. When the movement ceased, Hedges was squatting sideways on the crack in the door.

"You gonna cut your way out?" Forrest asked sardonically.

Hedges ignored him and took off his cap, wrapping it around the blade of the razor. Then he turned the instrument upside-down and pressed the handle between the door and the frame. He rested it against the underside of the iron bar that acted as a catch. He knew that if there was a padlock on the bar, he was beaten, but he hadn't heard any scrape of a key after the door was slid closed.

The car had become silent as the prisoners realized Hedges was attempting to find a way out. There was not now a trace of scorn on any of their faces as they peered through the near darkness towards the door. Some of them even showed a flickering of hope.

"When I lift this thing, you shove on the door," Hedges murmured to Forrest.

"I'm with you, Captain," the sergeant responded, and Hedges noted the revival of the title.

He gripped the protected blade in both hands and applied pressure. The bar was heavy, but he was working on the short end of it. He still had strength in reserve as the bar came free of its latch and stopped against the bracket.

"Shove," he rasped.

Forrest nodded, inserted his fingers into the crack and pushed. The door screeched on rusted runners, then was caught in the train's slipstream and rammed home to the limit of its travel. A great gust of fresh air and bright light filled the car. Men gulped and blinked their eyes. The fields of Georgia rushed by as a blur. Those prisoners who had been pressed against the door clung tenaciously to the men nearest them as the slipstream threatened to snatch them from the car. A babble of excited chatter rose but suddenly died down as the prisoners realized that leaping from the racketing train offered only an escape into death.

"Ain't no brake cord that I can see, Captain," Forrest pointed out acidly.

Hedges merely grunted in response, then climbed carefully to his feet, gripping the door frame as the slipstream buffeted him. When he reached up he found that he was just able to hook his fingertips over the edge of the car's flat roof. "You want to give me a boost?" he asked the sergeant, then turned his gaze towards Rhett.

"No copping a crafty feel, Bob," Forrest said as he wrapped an arm around one of Hedges' legs.

"He is rather butch," Rhett responded with an accentuated flickering of his eyelashes as he gripped the captain's other leg.

As other prisoners held the two men in position, they hoisted Hedges aloft. The slipstream plucked at Hedges clothing and stung his face as he folded his elbows onto the roof and hauled himself up, taking his weight off Forrest and Rhett.

"Okay?" a voice yelled from below.

"It's the only way to ride," he called as he stretched flat across the roof, looking first towards the front of the train, then the rear. He had seen six guards at the time he and his troopers were loaded on to the train, two coming from the camelback locomotive and four from the caboose: but the car door had been slammed before he was able to see if any changes were made.

But now, as he looked across the heaped logs in the tender, he saw that one more guard had chosen or been ordered to ride with the engineer and fireman. Another glance along the swaying car roofs towards the rear confirmed there was no immediate danger from this direction, and Hedges turned his body to a lengthwise position and began to inch forward. While the engineer concentrated upon his controls and the fireman rested from the arduous task of feeding logs into the fierce blaze, the three guards lounged in attitudes of bored disinterest, only one of them cradling a rifle—a French Le Faucheux. He and a second uniformed figure stared ahead to where the gleaming rails began a long curve around the foot of a bluff while the third guard peered across the open country spread out to the west of the track.

Just as the clatter of the moving train had masked the sound of Hedges' exit and the prisoners' reaction, so it covered the small scraping noises of the captain's belly-sliding progress along the roof of the car. His eyes squeezed almost shut against the streaming air, Hedges reached the leading edge of the car and snatched his attention away from the footplate for a moment to survey the gap between himself and the rear of the locomotive. It was about four feet.

Willing the guards and loco crew to continue with what engaged them, Hedges raised himself to his knees and then shuffled forward, fighting the pressure of the slipstream which threatened to knock him over backwards. Black wood smoke from the great inverted cone of the locomotive's stack disintegrated in the sunlit air above him, showering him with soot that clogged his ears and nostrils and burned his eyes. In the gap he could see the ties flashing by as a blur and the clack of the wheels was suddenly louder, emphasizing the inevitable death which awaited should he misjudge his move and drop on to the coupling, to be cannoned on to the track.

He fell forward, arms outstretched. His strong hands hooked over the rear of the tender, the impact sending a jarring pain along his arms to explode in his shoulders. He gritted his teeth, holding back a cry. His body swayed across the gap and held the position for several moments, concealed behind the heap of fuel logs. Then he pushed with his feet and pulled with his hands. His legs came clear of the car and his body folded down against the rear of the tender, his feet finding a firm hold on the coupling. The engineer sent the train roaring into the curve without slackening speed, opening a valve to emit a shrieking whistle.

Hedges paused only momentarily to regain his breath, then hoisted himself up on to the logs, peering over them towards the footplate, where all five men were now peering ahead as if anxious to see what lay around the curve. One man still cradled his six-shot revolving rifle. Hedges used the back of his hand to wipe soot from his eyes, then started down towards the front of the tender, the sharp corners of logs digging into his body.

The engineer was the first to sense danger and he whirled around, his grizzled features twisting into an expression of shock and fear. Hedges ignored him and the log he snatched up was directed towards the head of the guard with the rifle.

"Yankee!" the engineer yelled and the single word acted as a spring, whirling around the other men. The log smashed into the side of the guard's head, a corner stabbing deep into the eye and causing a spout of blood to issue forth, spraying into the face of the fireman.

As the guard crumpled, his rifle fell and bounced off the footplate to the side of the track. The fireman scrubbed frantically at his face with clenched fists, trying to wipe off the blood. Hedges sprang forward, right hand streaking towards the back of his neck. While the engineer was still petrified by shock, the two guards recovered and scrabbled for their holstered revolvers. Hedges crashed into one of them, spun him around and rested the honed edge of the razor against the pulsing side of his throat, locking the man's arms to his sides in a single-armed bear-hug. The third guard got his revolver clear of the holster and pointed it. His face showed indecision as he realized he could see little of Hedges but a great deal of his comrade.

Hedges showed his teeth in an icy grin. They shone whiter than ever against his soot-blackened face. "Bet you can blast him before I slice him," he said, shouting to be heard above the roaring wheezing of the Camelback.

"Drop it, Orville!" the threatened guard cried in alarm.

The revolver wavered. It was a ten-shot Walch with two hammers.

"Toss it," Hedges countermanded. "Over your head."

"You haven't got a chance," the guard warned.

"I'm an optimist," Hedges answered. "Toss it, feller."

"Orville!" the man in Hedges' power pleaded. "Do like he says."

The fireman was still trying to wipe himself clean of blood, spitting on his hands and massaging his face. The engineer was like a wax effigy, his frozen grip keeping the throttle wide open. The unconscious guard had not moved from where he had fallen. The man with the Walch stared hate at Hedges, then suddenly hurled the heavy revolver over his shoulder.

"I ain't sure I done the right thing Wilbur," he shouted, shaking his head.

"It was okay with me," Hedges said, releasing his grip on his prisoner and snatching the Starr .44 from the man's holster. He backed away, brandishing both the gun and the razor. The four men regarded him with fear and hate. The unconscious man groaned and twitched.

"What now?" Wilbur asked.

Hedges sidestepped, hooked a foot under the stomach of the injured guard and kicked out. The man, just beginning to gain control over his limp muscles, rolled off the edge of the footplate and thudded to the side of the track with a high, thin wail. The engineer found enough of his voice to emit a gasp.

"Your buddy did it the hard way," Hedges said with a vicious sneer contorting his mouth. "You got five seconds to pick your place. One."

"We'll be killed," Orville yelled.

"Give it a try," Hedges answered. "Two. Wave your arms. Maybe you'll fly. Three."

The train was round the foot of the bluff now and hurtling straight as an arrow along the edge of a pine forest with cotton fields on the other side. Wilbur moved gingerly to the side of the footplate and snatched a fearful glance over the edge. Hedges aimed the gun steadily at Orville, who scuttled to the side of his comrade.

"Four."

"There's a river ahead!" Wilbur yelled.

"You ain't got the time," Hedges said. "Five."

Both guards snatched a fast glance towards the Union captain, saw his finger tighten around the trigger, and launched themselves off the locomotive. Wilbur died instantly, smashing open his head against a telegraph pole. Orville broke both his legs as his feet crashed into the stump of a tree, then had his skull crushed beneath the leading car wheels as he bounced back across the track. The racketing note of the train altered as the locomotive hurtled across a trestle bridge above a slow-running river.

"You could have given them that chance," the engineer accused.

"Maybe you're right," Hedges allowed, sliding his razor back into its neck pouch. "Seems they weren't."

"Uh?"

"Didn't even try to fly. Stop the train, feller."

The engineer looked to left and right, licking the lips of his slack mouth. The fireman did the same; then Hedges. Each saw that the countryside had taken on a look of desolation and destruction. The pine forest had given way to an expanse of trampled brush growing in a tangled mass around the dead stumps that were all that remained of hundreds of felled trees. On the other side of the track was a deserted plantation, the fields overgrown with weeds; and the shacks of the Negro workers left to rot in a state of disrepair.

"Sure, Captain," the engineer answered, shooting a secretive glance at the fireman as he released the throttle and pulled hard on the brake handle.

Great billows of scalding steam hissed from valves and the wheels of the Camelback, screeched and showered sparks. Prison cars slammed into each other, straining their couplings and their tightly-packed occupants screamed in fear and bellowed in anger as the sudden braking flung them into struggling heaps of helpless humanity. Keeping the two-man crew covered, Hedges sprang forward to peer ahead.

"There's a depot!" he snapped. "Where is it?"

A triumphant smile curled up the corners of the engineer's slack mouth, but the fireman began to tremble. The engineer reached up and jerked down a cord. The high-pitched whistle screamed clearly above all the other noises of the slowing train.

"End of the line for you, Yankee," the man yelled gleefully. "Little place called Anderson. You made your play too late."

Hedges snarled and tilted the Starr. His curled trigger finger squeezed and the engineer screamed, dropping his hand from the whistle cord, blood oozing from a large hole drilled through the center of his palm. A roar of exaltation rose from a score of throats as the prisoners in the first car sprang through the open door, struggling to regain their balance as they hit the ground. The first to recover raced alongside the screeching train, leaping up to knock free the retaining bars on the doors of other cars.

The fireman saw the murderous look in Hedges' sooted face and leapt clear of the locomotive. He hit the ground, pitched forward and endeavored to scramble to his feet. Suddenly each of his arms was held in a strong grip and he was hauled clear of the ground. He looked in terror to left and right and saw the grinning faces of Seward and Bell.

"Don't!" he pleaded.

"Mine!" Seward shouted.

"Sure," Bell allowed and released his grip, falling back.

The fireman's legs folded beneath him and he was dragged along for two yards before Seward shoved him hard towards the train. He fell with a scream between two cars and a wheel sliced through him, cutting him cleanly in half with a sickening crunch of snapping bone.

The three guards leapt down from the caboose and went into a crouch, emptying their carbines towards the fleeing Union prisoners. Ten blue-clad figures fell, more than half of them dead, the remainder clawing at the dusty ground and screaming with the agony of their wounds. As the guards tossed aside their carbines and reached for side irons, the prisoners nearest to them turned and rushed them. One guard fired a single shot, turning the revolver towards his own head as he saw the intent upon the faces of the attacking

103

prisoners. The other two were toppled backwards by the onrush and did not have time to scream. Fists and boots smashed into their flesh. Fingers gouged and nails scratched. When the Union men stood up the guards were no more than pulpy masses of bleeding flesh clothed in the shreds of uniforms.

As the train at last ground to a halt, the initial exhilaration of escape left the prisoners. Many were already far across the ruined fields and denuded forest. Now those who had held back to take part in the slaughter of the guards turned and streamed away, their pace quickening as a volley of rifle fire crackled out from the direction of the Anderson depot.

"We go back," Hedges snarled at the engineer who was whimpering as he pressed his shattered hand against his side.

"You'll never make it," the man hissed between clenched teeth.

Hedges lashed out with the Starr and the engineer reeled back with a scream, pouring blood from his mouth where the sight of the revolver had opened his top gum. The rifle fire was louder. Some wild bullets clanged against the locomotive. One of them ricocheted off the smokestack and tore into the throat of the engineer. The man fell backwards off the footplate and thudded to add his lifeless body to the many that littered the side of the track.

Hedges cursed and turned to survey the controls and gauges arrayed across the front of the cab.

"These iron horses ain't as easy as the four-legged kind are they, Yankee?"

Hedges whirled, levelling the Starr, then allowed the gun to slip from his grasp as he saw the muzzle of the Springfield rifle unwaveringly trained upon the center of his stomach. It was in the hands of a mounted Confederate cavalry lieutenant who appeared anxious to use the weapon.

"Sure don't react to giddy-up," Hedges answered evenly, looking across the shoulder of his captor to where more than a hundred mounted calvary and infantrymen were in hot pursuit of the fleeing prisoners.

"Get down here," the lieutenant ordered, backing off his horse, but keeping the rifle steady on its target. "Boy, is Captain Wirz going to enjoy having you in Andersonville."

Hedges took his time climbing down from the locomotive and the lieutenant appeared to be in no hurry. Unlike many other rebel soldiers who had overhauled the prisoners and were forcing them back towards the railroad on the run, urging them onwards with the prod of rifle muzzles in their backs.

"Why me, lieutenant?" Hedges asked, gathering some saliva in his mouth, swirling it around to soak up the soot and spitting it out.

"He don't like troublemakers," the rebel trooper answered. "He's got permanent gut aches and a Yankee near shot off his arm at Seven Pines. Both play him up worse when there's trouble. Let's go."

A jerk of the head indicated the direction. The turning of Hedges's body altered the aim of the rifle from his stomach to the center of his back. As he ambled along beside the railroad, he was joined by other prisoners, breathless and disconsolate in their failure to escape. As the group swelled, the captors fell back and wide to the sides, rifles at the ready for the first sign of trouble. A man pushed forward through the group and fell into pace beside Hedges.

"Ain't our day, is it, Captain?" Forrest said grimly.

Hedges looked around him and saw that the group of prisoners was swelling by the moment. Beyond, on both sides of the gleaming rails, were the slumped figures of those prisoners who had been killed by the rebels. If any Union men had escaped recapture or death, they were few.

"You want me to say I was wrong to try it, Sergeant?" Hedges said, returning his gaze to the face of Forrest.

Forrest shook his head, his mouth cracking in a grin. "Men like you and me, we're only ever wrong once. And we ain't alive to have any regrets."

"Close up in columns of threes!" An order rang out and those who were slow to respond were urged into compliance with rifle butts swung by grim-faced troopers. "Go to the left, left!"

The head of the column swung into a turn, urged by the levelled muskets of a line of infantrymen, bypassing the tiny village of Anderson huddled around the small South Western Railroad depot and heading along a road across a swamp towards the fifteen feet high pine fence of Andersonville's stockade.

The level of misery to which the spirits of many prisoners sunk at the sight of the Confederate prison was deepened by the awareness of how close they had been to escaping the fate which awaited them behind the impassive fence. But Hedges was unperturbed by this new turn of events. As Forrest had pointed out, he was still alive and while he continued to be so he was on the winning side.

The column straggled past one of the four forts that guarded the prison, then the cookhouse and the bakery, the smell of burning food mingling with the heavier odors rising from the swamp which steamed lazily in the hot Georgia sun.

The road dead-ended against a heavy gate, but as the prisoners and their escort approached, two guards moved forward and swung the barrier aside. As the prisoners ambled through, the escorting soldiers sheered away.

"Welcome, Yankees," a pale-faced, red-eyed little guard in a too-large uniform yelled gleefully. "Make yourselves at home."

"Shut your stupid mouth, Mint Julep," a second guard bellowed, running his cruel eyes over the new group of prisoners come to experience the misery which had already been the lot of thousands of other Union soldiers with the ill luck to fall into Confederate hands.

*　*　*

"You were a guard at Andersonville!" Edge said, snapping out of his reverie and sitting up suddenly, pointing a finger like a revolver barrel towards the prisoner in the next cell.

Mint Julep was sitting on his mattress, clasping his knees to his chest, fingers entwined in front of his calves. His face was haggard and his eyes sunken as he suffered the effects of enforced abstenance. "It weren't so clean as this place, but at least I could get a drink there," he muttered absently.

Edge shook his head, clearing it of the last vestiges of thoughts from out of the past. The movement set off renewed pain from his bruised head, but the sensation was less intense than it had been before. He stood up and stretched, feeling the razor pouch pressing against his neck. It was hot in the jailhouse and his underwear was tacky against his skin. He rested his hands on the bars of the cell and looked at the sleeping hulk of Marshal Railston sprawled in the chair behind the desk.

"Sure ain't no sleeping beauty, is he?" Mint Julep said. "Resting that way he looks meaner than when he's awake."

"What about his deputy?" Edge asked.

"Vic ain't mean," the suffering drunk answered. "He's a straight guy. Ain't many lawmen like him around, I'm telling you."

Edge returned to the bunk and sat down, taking off

his hat and using it to fan his sweating face. The motion merely stirred the humid air without cooling it.

"Hey, mister?"

Edge looked through the bars at Mint Julep. "Yeah?"

"I do you any harm at Andersonville?" A dry tongue licked drier lips.

"Not that I recall," Edge answered.

"Appreciate it if you wouldn't put the word around—about me being a sentry there, I mean. Lot of Yank . . . Northerners got long memories about what happened down there in Georgia. Figure we was all the same. I never hurt nobody. Some people wouldn't believe that." He sought to moisten his lips again and failed. "They'd make trouble for me, you know?"

"I got enough trouble of my own," Edge told him.

"Thanks," Mint Julep said, the single word filled with genuine feeling.

A horse clip-clopped into the yard behind the jailhouse and a man's voice spoke softly to it as leather slapped against the wood of a hitching rail. As Deputy Paxton entered the marshal's office his face showed the fatigue compounded of lack of sleep the previous night and the exhausting heat of the day. But he seemed to gain some relief from the sight of the sleeping Railston. Hedges watched the young deputy cautiously as Paxton crossed the office on the points of his riding boots and halted at the cell door. Paxton threw a glance over his shoulder to check on the red-headed marshal before speaking in a low tone.

"Emmeline Greer's holed up somewhere in the Garden of Eden," he said.

Both Edge and Mint Julep got off their bunks and moved to the front of their cells, as if each had an equal interest in Paxton's information.

"Is that the way she wants it to be?" Edge asked.

Paxton shook his head. "I don't think so. I heard Lydia Eden talking with Red. It seems he wants to get rid of her, but the old lady is happy to keep her under wraps until after the trial."

Edge narrowed his eyes and looked hard into Paxton's young face. "What you going to do about it?"

"It's a mighty big property," Paxton answered with a tired sigh.

"I know it pretty good," Mint Julep put in quickly, and loudly.

The marshal groaned and his chair creaked as he changed position in his sleep. The drunk flinched back from the hard glares of Edge and the deputy.

"How come?" Paxton asked.

Mint Julep's voice became a hoarse whisper. "Real plump jackrabbits skipping around that place. Sometimes I set gins and catch me a few to sell."

"That's dangerous," Paxton said.

The drunk grimaced. "Going without eating and drinking is a damn sight more dangerous, Mr. Paxton," he pointed out. "You get any clue as to whereabouts they got the whore?"

Paxton shrugged. "The Garden of Eden has got a long ocean frontage. Lydia Eden mentioned a beach-house."

The drunk's wizened face lit with a grin. He seemed about to burst forth with a revelation, but a flash of Edge's eyes cautioned him into a low tone. "I know where that is," he said quickly.

"Don't keep it no secret," Edge said coldly.

Mint Julep blinked and ran a fingernail down one of the bars separating his cell from that of Edge—as if to test that it really was made of unbending iron. "What's it worth to me?" he asked lightly.

Edge's burnished features formed into a snarling expression. He spoke through clenched teeth. "What did you do in the war, Daddy?" he hissed.

The drunk swallowed hard.

"I'll get a bottle of wine in to you," Paxton said, failing to understand why Mint Julep was more impressed by Edge's strange comment than the promise of liquor.

"You ain't no honorable man, mister," Mint Julep said sadly.

"They want to hang me tomorrow," Edge said softly. "I don't give one damn about my honor, so long as my neck stays intact."

"About a mile up the shoreline from the south boundary marker," Mint Julep said, trying to ignore Edge as he spoke directly to Paxton. "On a shelf of rock above the beach. Stairway goes up to it from the dunes. I'd sure appreciate that bottle, young feller."

Paxton nodded his acknowledgement, then looked at Edge. "I can't make her tell it your way," he said earnestly.

"Just get her into the courtroom," Edge told him.

Paxton sighed. "I'll leave it till tonight. Lydia Eden's trigger-happy guards will have less chance to spot me."

"Better get that bottle while the bastard's still napping, Mr. Paxton," Mint Julep urged, hugging himself to try to stop a new bout of trembling.

"Sure thing," Paxton said and turned to leave the jailhouse as quietly as he had entered.

Both prisoners returned to their bunks and regarded each other through the bars of the partition.

"They were bad times," Mint Julep said when the silence became unbearable to him. "In that place."

"You won't find nobody to disagree with you," Edge replied.

"That Henry Wirz," the drunk muttered, shaking his head from side to side. "He was probably meaner than even Red Railston."

"He was a German, wasn't he?"

"From someplace in Europe. He talked funny. Not like an American."

"German, I reckon," Edge said. "He sure had ways of making us talk."

CHAPTER SEVEN

Captain Henry Wirz, commandant of Andersonville Prison was, in fact, a native of Zurich in German-speaking Switzerland. But both in his bearing and his speech he was strongly influenced by things Prussian and as he strutted through the stockade's north gate that afternoon there was about him an arrogance which was part inbred and part affected. For he wore his attitude as a cloak to conceal his deep frustrations. In his early forties, he was a round-shouldered man with a sallow skin and bloodshot eyes. Most of the time he was in pain from a dyspeptic stomach and an arm wound received during a battle near Richmond. But the agony he suffered in the mind was far harder to bear than mere physical discomfort. For Wirz was a proud man who considered he deserved a superior rank to that of captain and a more rewarding post than the one he had.

It was, therefore, perhaps understandable that the luckless Union prisoners in Andersonville received the backlash of the commandant's dissatisfaction. And on that afternoon, one particular prisoner bore the brunt of Wirz's cruelty born of frustration.

Under the menacing muskets of the guards, three

Negroes had erected a framework of two upright posts with a cross member some ten feet from the ground on one side of the prison track called Main Street. Stripped to the waist, Hedges had been given the choice of being shot or allowing himself to be strung from the cross member by ropes tied around his wrists. For an hour he had hung there, at first able to watch with near detachment as the other prisoners were rounded up by brutal guards and organized into disorderly ranks to form three sides of a square in front and at the sides of him. But then the beating heat of the sun on his bare head and the strain of supporting his own body weight had begun to take its toll.

Moisture oozed from every pore of his body, beginning to form into rivulets across his coppery skin but almost at once becoming tacky and then drying to salt which built up into a stinging crust. And soon there was no more sweat to be drawn; to the man it seemed that even the blood had been drained from him by the harsh Georgia sun. His skin began to burn, showing patches of angry redness that soon developed white blisters. Parallelling the expanding pain of his dehydration, Hedges experienced an upward curve of torturing agony which began at his shoulder blades and progressed by degrees along his arms until even the very tips of his fingers were screaming for release.

But no sound sprang from his lips, which gradually curled back to show his teeth in a silent snarl while the pain mirrored in his eyes was blanketed by lids screwed tight shut. Thus, by the time that the more than three thousand Union prisoners were in position, Hedges was no longer aware of their presence as he fought with an iron will to turn all his senses inwards and concentrate his diminishing strength upon containing the urgent need to plead for mercy.

"You will now confess your actions and give your word of honor to obey the laws of this establishment for the duration of your stay."

Wirz had halted before the framework and was staring up into the mask of agony that had spread across Hedges' face. He spoke slowly and distinctly and when he received no response he lifted his gold-headed walking cane and jabbed it viciously into the captive's navel. The thrust was hard enough to set Hedges' suffering was the most powerful personifica-broke through the defence of a mental block he had erected so earnestly. His eyes snapped open and a low groan erupted from his throat and hissed between his tightly clamped teeth. He raised his chin from his chest and moved his head from side to side. His vision was blurred by a scarlet mist of agony: but he knew the vista from the memory of the first few minutes of suffering.

Row upon row of wretched humanity ranged against a background of a swampy enclosure of firmly embedded pine logs, littered in tightly packed disorder with ragged tents and crude shacks. It was a panorama of misery, the whole drawing from each individual experience so that while the potent example of Hedges' suffering was the most powerful personification of Andersonville's anguish, it generated little sympathy from the reluctant audience. For slow death and crippling disease were as much inmates of the prison as the captured men, and compassion for another's torment diminished as a man's own misery increased.

"You will confess escaping—leading the escape—and murdering two civilians and six men of the Confederate Army, Captain."

Hedges looked through the opaqueness of his eyes into the thin, cruel face of Wirz. "What's the reward?" he croaked.

113

The yellow tinge of the commandant's skin deepened as rage swept over him. Hedges screwed his eyes closed again and pressed his swollen tongue against the roof of his mouth to hold back a cry as his body ceased to swing and seemed to grow heavier by the moment.

"A confession is its own reward," Wirz snapped. "Your punishment will be decided later."

Hedges sucked from deep in his throat, seeking a drain of moisture to lubricate his mouth. "You know already," he managed to rasp.

Wirz looked around at the assembled prisoners, enjoying their emaciation, the hatred shining dully from their hollow eyes, the filth clinging to their ragged uniforms, the stench emanating from bodies.

"I know," he replied, speaking to the prisoners. "But these creatures do not. This rabble believes no word I speak, so they must hear from you why you are being punished. They must be taught that I am a just man."

"You're nothing but crud," John Scott muttered, then screamed and pitched forward, clutching at his groin.

One of several guards on the ground, augmenting the protection given by many more on the stockade wall, had heard Scott's insult and stepped forward, swinging his carbine hard and accurately.

"Christ!" Rhett exclaimed, but bit off further words as a beefy guard swung towards him.

The new batch of prisoners were grouped together, their freshness to Andersonville evident from the comparative neatness of their uniforms and the well-fed look of their faces and bellies.

"Nobody talks while the captain's speaking," the guard snarled at Rhett who drew back, beginning to tremble.

Scott clawed at the dusty ground and moaned his pain. The guard who had floored him raised his carbine again and brought it down, stock first. Polished wood crunched against Scott's skull and the Union trooper rolled onto his back and was silent. On the other side of the road a boy of eighteen with cheekbones that seemed about to break through the slack greyness of his skin clutched at his stomach and collapsed, his bowels vacating the stench of untreated dysentery. The prisoners and guards close to him shuffled away. Flies swarmed in and settled on the dying boy.

"Get yourself another teacher," Hedges rasped.

Wirz stepped to the side, raising his cane. His knuckles were white around the head as he swung the heavy wood. It landed across Hedges' lower stomach with a resounding smack that forced a cry from the captive and caused him to jerk up his knees. When his legs straightened they felt like lead weights and their heaviness only heightened the burning pain.

"This man is a fool!" Wirz screamed at the rows of prisoners. "Had he agreed to confess his crime he would have been cut down and given water. He chooses to be obstinate. For this his punishment will be prolonged. He will stay where he is until sundown. If any prisoner comes within ten yards of him, that prisoner will be shot."

Wirz stooped down and scraped up a handful of dust. Then he reversed his cane, grasping it tightly with the hand of his good arm. "You and you," he snapped, stabbing the cane towards two guards. "A leg each. Open them."

The designated men sprang forward and did as commanded, drawing Hedges' legs wide apart. Hedges opened his eyes and saw Wirz as a mere dark shadow against the blazing whiteness of the ground. For a moment he believed he was to be cut down, but it was a fleeting error.

The gold head of the cane flashed in the sunlight as it travelled in an underarm arc. Blazing agony exploded and scattered to every nerve in Hedges' body as the blow landed. The opaqueness in front of his eyes began to revolve and he heard a scream without realizing it sprang from his own lips. His mouth and eyes were pulled wide. Wirz hurled the dust and Hedges felt it swirl into his mouth and clog his nostrils and eyes. The shadowed world began to turn more quickly, then became streaked with brilliant flashes of light, like a multicolored thunderstorm.

"I hope you die," a Germanic voice hissed a moment before the lights went out, the shadows merged into darkness and Hedges dived off the springboard of pain into the soothing sea of unconsciousness.

The level of his senselessness wavered throughout the remainder of the day and sometimes an involuntary sound issued from his slack mouth. But on each occasion when he neared the edge of waking his mind refused to accept the burden of pain and drove him back into the deep darkness. Around him, prison camp life returned to normal. One man collapsed from malnutrition and pitched headfirst into the ill-named Sweetwater Creek which cut a course through the swamp at the center of the compound. He drowned before anybody took the trouble to haul him out. Two men who had been wounded just before capture finally succumbed to the gangrene. A boy soldier who had been on the same prison train as Hedges tried to protect his near-new boots from one of the many gangs of marauding raiders which made periodic assaults on fellow prisoners. He was beaten to death with sticks, but not before the raiders had stripped him of his clothing. Bodies were either left where they fell or dragged clear of living quarters to await the call of the dead wagon the following morning. Guards patrolled the stockade wall and kept watch from sentry towers, hardened to the conditions before their bored gazes.

Not until the last redness had faded from the western sky did the lieutenant of the watch issue an order to a sergeant. This sergeant, with a six-man escort, went into the compound through the north gate. A few prisoners watched the activity, but most ignored it. While four guards fanned the surrounding area with their carbines, two others hoisted the captain onto their shoulders.

"He still alive, Sarge?" a man asked.

"You care?" the non-com asked.

The man shrugged.

The sergeant sawed through one rope and Hedge's body sagged, swinging and turning as he hung by the right arm. "Cut him down, the snotnose officer told me," the sergeant said sourly as he hacked at the second rope. "So I ain't about to start feeling if his ticker's still pumping."

The final strand of the rope parted and Hedge's inert body slumped hard to the ground.

"One thing's for sure," a guard commented as the sergeant was lowered. "He ain't the healthiest Yankee we got here."

Dusk had fallen heavily and there was a palpable menace in the shadowed darkness within the compound. Each man in the detail experienced a throat-drying fear as he moved towards the gate, eyes raking over the untidy rows of sagging shelters.

"The bogey man will get you, rebs," a voice called from the left.

"Yeah," a shout emerged from the right. "He'll come and stick a knife in your guts and keep twisting it until you've got nothing behind your belly button 'cepting bad gas."

"It's all they got there now," a third voice yelled tauntingly. "Every Johnny Reb lost his guts first time he saw a blue uniform."

High, desperate laughter trickled around the stockade and the rebel detail broke into a run and breathed a heartfelt sigh of relief as one man when they crossed over the deadline—a length of twine which ran parallel with each wall and which prisoners stepped over on penalty of immediate shooting by guards on the wall.

Not until the north gate had been slammed closed did a five-man group of prisoners cross Main Street and crouch down beside the crumpled form of Hedges.

"He ain't breathing, looks like," Bill Seward said flatly.

"He's breathing," Forrest snapped, bending close to Hedges' face and detecting the faint draught of expelled air from the open mouth of the unconscious man. "Hal and Johnny, carry him. Gentle-like. Bob, go get some fresh water."

"Where?" Rhett asked helplessly, with a nervous glance around the darkened compound.

Forrest stood and leaned close to the New Englander, who took a step backwards under the steelly stare of the sergeant. "First you try the creek," Forrest hissed venomously. "If that's fouled, maybe there's a spring around. If you strike out there, find another fag and sell your ass for a bucket of water."

"Christ, Frank," Rhett said miserably.

"All else fails," Forrest went on, ignoring the comment, "you get down on your hands and knees and you either pray for rain or dig a well. You bring me back some water, or I'll wring you out with my bare hands. That oughta get us a couple of gallons."

Rhett nodded vigorously. "Where'll I bring it, Frank?"

Forrest looked up and down Main Street, then pointed. "Last shebang on the left."

"How you know it ain't taken?"

Forrest spat. "Get lost, Bob," he muttered. "Leave men to do men's work."

Rhett was about to offer a retort, but saw the cold glint in Forrest's eyes and moved nervously away into the darkness. Then Forrest held out his hand towards Seward. "The Captain's blade, Billy?" he asked.

When Hedges had been ordered to strip to the waist, he was careful to untie the cord of the neck pouch and slide the weapon and its container off with his shirt. Then he had screwed up the shirt around the razor and handed it with his tunic and undervest to the man closest to him. Seward had been the recipient. It was with some reluctance that the youngster took the closed razor from his pocket and gave it to Forrest.

"What'd you do with his other stuff?"

"The clothes is hid," Seward answered. He looked at the ground and kicked up dust with the edge of a boot. "If he croaks, do I get the blade back? He gave it to me, Frank."

Forrest's mouth cracked in a grin. "You ever known me give anything to anyone, Billy?"

Seward sighed.

"Let's move," Forrest said, and led the way along Main Street. Seward fell in behind him with Douglas and Bell bringing up the rear swinging the burden of Hedges between them.

The shelter Forrest had selected had three wooden sides and one of tin, with a piece of canvas stretched across the top as a roof. There was no door: merely a hole to crawl through in one of the wooden sides. As Forrest stooped down to peer inside, a vile odor compounded of excrement, urine, sweat and stale air assaulted his nostrils.

"Anyone in this stinkhole?" he demanded.

"That Olsen?" a small voice whined. "I need some bad, Olsen."

A pale blur appeared at the hole and became recognizable as a man's face when Forrest reached in, grabbed a handful of shirt front and yanked the occupant of the shelter into the open. He looked fifty but may have been twenty. His face was skeletal in its thinness so that his dark-rimmed eyes seemed to be sunk deep beneath his jutting brows and the dirt-grimed skin followed closely every rise and indentation of his bone structure. His head was completely bald but at first glance in the darkness seemed not to be so, because of the many scabbed and fresh sores which covered his skull.

"You're not Olsen," he said, disappointed rather than fearful as he looked up into Forrest's cruel face.

"I ain't," Forrest agreed. "Just you in here?"

The wretched man nodded. "Just old West Point himself. There were two others. They had the craps all the time. They died. Went out on the dead wagon. That's what I'm going to do. I went to West Point, you know that? I'm going back there. I'm getting out on the dead wagon. Only I won't be dead."

The man began to giggle, but the sound became a hacking cough. Forrest transferred his grip to the back of the man's neck and hauled him completely out of the shelter. He beckoned for Bell and Douglas to ease Hedges inside.

"Looks like he's for the dead wagon," West Point said as the bout of coughing finished. "But he's dead and that's not the way."

He began to shake his festering head from side to side, his thin features forming into a shallow frown.

"He's as crazy as a loon," Seward said scornfully.

"He's got it made," Forrest answered. "First man I've seen in this joint who can laugh." He looked around. "Go find lover boy, Billy. Sight of all these guys cooped up with nowhere to run might have gone to *his* head."

120

As Seward moved away, Forrest crawled through into the shelter, meeting the full brunt of the stench. There was no form of bed inside and Hedges was stretched out on his back on the bare earth. Forrest ordered Bell to take off his tunic and fold it to use for a pillow.

"Why we doing this, Frank?" Douglas wanted to know.

Forrest snorted. "You know any way out of this pigpen, Hal?"

"Hell, there ain't no way," Douglas answered bitterly.

"That's how it looks for sure," Forrest concurred, and pointed a finger at Hedges, "But if we can pull him through, he won't see it that way. Just like every other guy in here, he'll want out. But what the Captain wants, he gets some way or other. Because he's got brains and he knows how to use them. He won't just want—he'll get. And we'll get with him."

There was a shuffling sound behind Forrest and he turned, expecting to see Rhett or Seward. But it was the evicted West Point who stared back at him.

"Olsen's coming," the old-young man announced with a tone of excitement. "You want anything?"

"Who's Olsen?" Forrest demanded.

"He's The Man," West Point answered, speaking in capitals. "You want any morphine, heroin, extra rations, get a letter out—anything. Olsen can fix it."

"Move the butt, West Point," a voice roared from outside, and the man in the entrance was suddenly shot forward, propelled by a boot landed heavily on his rump. A lantern was thrust into the shelter and then the man holding it followed the light inside. "Ah," he said with a sigh as he sat down crosslegged on the dirt floor. "New customers for the store. Glad to meet you, gents. Name's Olsen. Bringer of comforts in these days of deprivation. Have it now and pay for it later."

The three new prisoners looked at Olsen in open-mouthed amazement, astonished by the contrast he presented to the thousands of other Union men they had seen in the stockade. For Olsen was fat to the extent of obesity; he was clean-shaven and recently washed and his clothes comprised an Eastern business suit complete with matching grey derby. He was a rotund man with a round, angelic face shiny with health in the yellow glow of the kerosene lamp and his small, bright green eyes were alive with vitality.

Forrest was the first to recover and his voice was a snarl. "What do you want, punk?" he demanded.

Olsen was unperturbed by the insult. "I want nothing. I came to supply West Point with what he requires." A knowing smile flitted across his complacent expression. "You men are new. In time you will discover you have requirements, too."

The fat man took a small bottle from his inside pocket and held it out. West Point made a grab for it with a filthy hand which was merely a pattern of bones hung with skin. "I got my marker made out already, Olsen," the little wretch screeched, scrabbling inside his ragged shirt and pulling out a slip of paper. "Twenty-five dollars, right?"

Olsen smiled, nodded, took the paper and released the bottle. West Point had to work hard at unscrewing the cap. He shook out four tablets and swallowed them like a starving animal taking food.

"What's that junk?" Forrest demanded.

"Hardly that," Olsen answered. "Poor West Point was shot in the head at Antietam Creek. The surgeon gave him morphine to kill the pain. Unfortunately, he became addicted to it. Latest medical evidence suggests that a new drug called heroin will cure addiction. It doesn't seem to be working for West Point, but it keeps him happy."

"I still say it's junk," Forrest snapped.

Olsen shrugged. "It might catch on. Who knows?

Can I get anything for you or your unfortunate friend?"

"You can get lost," Forrest replied.

"I'll be around if you change your mind," Olsen said, beginning to slide out of the shelter, and reaching for the lamp.

Forrest leaned forward sharply and applied a vise-like grip around Olsen's wrist. "Leave the light."

"I can get you one for fifty dollars." Olsen said, wincing as Forrest applied more pressure to his wrist.

The razor appeared in Forrest's free hand and he flicked out the blade with a sudden wrist action. "You can get dead for nothing," he hissed, placing the blade beneath's Olsen's double chin and forcing the man's head up to look in his eyes.

"You're making a mistake," the fat man said with a tremor in his voice.

Forrest showed him his teeth. "It's cheaper than making an offer."

"I've got friends."

"Ain't no use to you dead, mister."

Olsen swallowed hard. The action caused his flabby chins to move and the razor nicked the skin. "An introductory gift," he rasped.

"We don't want charity," Forrest muttered, removing the razor from its dangerous position. "You get your life in exchange."

Olsen was already half out of the hole in the wall. Forrest placed the heel of his hand against the fat man's forehead and shoved hard. Olsen was ejected into the night with a squeal.

"You didn't oughta have done that," West Point said, aghast. "He'll make trouble."

Forrest whirled towards the little man, but held back a retort as he saw the tablets were taking their effect, spreading an imbecilic grin across the starved face, heightening the impression of a skull. He turned back to look at Hedges, drawing the lamp closer. The determination in his eyes was not tempered by compassion as he examined the salt-crusted face of the unconscious man and roved over the blistered body with an ugly red welt across the base of the stomach where the cane had made contact. But there was a mere flicker of anxiety visible as the sergeant felt for a pulse and for a moment failed to detect the tiny beat at the reddened side of Hedges' neck.

Rhett crawled in through the hole first, a pail of water clutched in his trembling hands. Scott came in behind him, bleary-eyed and with dried blood encrusting one side of his face. Seward brought up the rear, his young face heavy with anger. Forrest snatched the pail and then ripped the kerchief from Rhett's neck.

"Took you goddam long enough," the sergeant snarled.

Rhett scuttled into a corner and looked fearfully from Forrest to Seward, like a terrified animal. Forrest folded the kerchief, soaked it and began to bathe Hedges' face and body.

"He's crazier than that nut," Seward sneered, nodding towards the grinning West Point. 'I found him going from one tent to another asking for the loan of a pail of water—like some city woman on the cadge for a cup of sugar."

"Where'd you get it, Billy?" Bell asked.

Seward's anger was suddenly gone and was replaced by a look of proud cunning. "We found Johnnie and made him play dead. While Bob made like he wanted to sell Johnnie's boots and gear to a group of guys, I sneaked into their hut and swiped it."

Rhett sought to return to favor and forced a guffaw. "You should have seen their faces when Johnnie suddenly came alive and we all started to run like hell."

The rest, with the exception of Forrest and the unconscious Hedges, joined in his amusement and other prisoners and guards alike who were within earshot of the shelter turned confused eyes towards the source of the hilarity. For laughter was an alien sound within the stockade. But then somebody pointed out the glee was emitting from West Point's shelter.

"Birds of a feather," a veteran guard commented to a companion. "Guess some of the new guys came in minus their marbles."

The young corporal leaning beside him suddenly laughed. "Gave themselves up, you reckon?"

"Uh?"

"Asked for asylum?"

* * *

Deputy Paxton galloped his horse along the firmly packed sand of the shoreline, sometimes kicking up spray as a breaking wave, more adventurous than others, carried its assault higher up the beach. And within moments of his passing, the advance of the tide wiped out every trace of his presence.

It was after midnight and Paxton was a lonely figure in the darkness which was slightly silvered by a waning moon hanging low in the sky. It seemed to be the only light in the world, for the city was far behind him and the rising ground of the Garden of Eden spread to one side was as desolate as the vacant ocean to the other.

But then, as the young deputy stared ahead, something flashed from out of the shadowed area of a cliff face and he reined his mount to a walking pace. The horse snorted and breathed deeply of the salty clean air. Paxton spoke softly to the animal and caressed its neck as he studied the cliff; and as he drew closer his facial muscles tightened into an expression of part nervousness, part satisfaction. For he could see the silhouette of a small house, the dark pine wood of its construction set against the faintly whitish tinge of the cliff face. The flash had been moonlight reflected off a window pane.

He angled his mount away from the shoreline, the animal's legs sinking deep into the soft sand, and hitched the reins around a hooklike projection of rock at the foot of the cliff. He was a hundred feet short of the wooden stairway reaching up to the shelf upon which the house was built, and did not draw his Colt until he started up the steps. He made the top quickly and quietly, and there confirmed his first impression that no lights burned behind the four front windows of the one-story building. But he hesitated as he saw that the door was open.

"You stopped at the right place," a voice said from within the house. "One more step and I'd have blown your heart out."

Paxton's stomach turned to ice-cold water. He leaned forward slightly, straining his eyes to penetrate the velvet blackness inside the doorway.

"Drop the gun, kid."

Paxton's muscles wouldn't obey the dictates of his mind. He had to bring his left hand across the front of his body to unfold his fingers from around the revolver. It clunked to the ground. A tall, thin man stepped out of the doorway, his eyes and teeth shining in the moonlight. The star on his vest gleamed more brightly. He was aiming a Winchester at Paxton.

"Jesus, you're Red Railston's deputy," the man said, dropping the rifle's aim to the ground.

Paxton's pent-up breath escaped with a hiss but he waited for several moments before he risked speaking. Even so, the words seemed to him to have an unnatural sound. "You get your star through mail order?"

The man looked tough, but unintelligent. He shook

his head. "Mrs. Eden had the marshal deputize us. We're guarding a material witness in the Chadwick Eden case."

The plural form was confirmed as a second man emerged from the house. He looked tougher and more stupid than his partner. He was broader, but shorter. He also wore a star.

Paxton's mind raced. "Red wants the girl at the jailhouse," he said.

"We like having here here," the second man answered.

"He don't mean that like it sounds," the first explained nervously. "She ain't been touched."

"He got authority?" the second man asked, eyeing Paxton with suspicion.

"He's a regular deputy, Ed. I reckon he don't need it."

Paxton thought it was safe to retrieve his gun, and he scooped it up. He held it loosely in his hand, aimed at nowhere, but ready.

"Mrs. Eden ought to know about it," Ed said. "You go tell her, Slim."

Ed dropped a hand to his holstered Starr. Paxton levelled the Colt.

Slim licked his lips, made to raise the Winchester and decided against it. "Frisco law don't mean nothing here, mister."

Paxton hefted the Colt. "You want to argue with this law?"

"He won't shoot," Ed said.

"Try me," Paxton told him, and raised his voice. "Miss Greer!"

There was a creak of bedsprings and then the padding of bare feet on polished wood. The voluptuous form of the whore appeared in the doorway, clothed in a voluminous nightgown. Her face was heavy with sleep and aged by a lack of make-up.

127

"Ain't two men enough?" she asked irritably.

"You like it here?" Paxton asked her.

She sneered towards Slim and Ed. "You must be kidding. I didn't know there were so many snakes in the Garden of Eden."

"Get your clothes on."

"I'm going with you?"

Paxton's confidence increased for he knew the woman would be disappointed if he gave her a negative answer. He nodded.

She smiled. "Where we going?"

"Back to San Francisco."

The smile broadened. "That's my town."

"Figured it was where you left your heart," he told her as she turned to re-enter the house. "Toss your guns down on the beach," he said to Slim and Ed.

"Mrs. Eden won't like this," Slim complained.

"Everything in the garden can't always be rosy," Paxton answered. "Toss them."

Slim shrugged and threw the Winchester over the edge of the shelf. He wore no gunbelt. Ed eased out the Starr and was careful to hold it by the barrel. He arced it away into the night.

"You don't look dead, but you are," he rasped at Paxton.

"Back up," the young deputy told them, jerking the Colt. The two moved along to the corner of the house, furthest from the head of the stairway. Emmeline Greer came out, still buttoning her dress over her ample bosom. "Down the steps," he instructed and she hurried to obey.

Paxton went down more slowly, sideways on so that he could keep Ed and Slim covered. She was waiting on the beach.

"We going to walk, mister?"

"I got one horse," he answered.

She grinned as she fell into step beside him. "Good, I like riding with a man."

"Reckoned you would," he said as they reached the tethered animal and he helped her to swing up behind the saddle. He didn't holster the Colt until he was mounted and had heeled the horse into a canter, heading across the beach to the firmness at the tideline. "You haven't asked why I got you away, Miss Greer," he called over his shoulder as she tightened her encircling arms about his waist.

"It ain't germane," she said with a laugh. "I'm just so happy to be liberated."

They galloped south through the shattered remains of the breaking surf.

CHAPTER EIGHT

It took Hedges six weeks to fully recover from the effects of his initiation into Andersonville and by that time Forrest was beginning to adopt an attitude similar to the one shared by the other five Union troopers who had commandeered West Point's shack. For the captain gave no hint that he had any intention of trying to escape from the awful conditions under which they were all held prisoner. But, fortunately for Hedges, the sergeant's disenchantment did not take effect until after the injured man was well enough to survive without help.

"He talks too much to the nutter," Bell said sourly one evening as he and Forrest were relieving themselves into the edge of the swamp. "I reckon he's cracking up, Frank. They just sit around and gab all day."

Forrest grimaced and buttoned his fly. Then he retied the length of cord that he used to keep his pants up since he had traded his belt for a pouch of tobacco, making the deal with the alcoholic guard known to everyone as Mint Julep. He needed less of the cord's length each day as his girth narrowed, the meager ration of cornmeal taking its weakening effect. "Maybe I should have let him croak and cut him up for steaks."

Bell, thinner and more hollow-eyed than the sergeant, sighed reflectively. "I heard some guys over near the south deadline caught a dog and cooked him. Said it tasted like prime beef fresh off the hoof."

The two men began to head back for the shelter, unresponsive to the groans of prisoners suffering slow, diseased death in their stinking shebangs. A prisoner showing his ribcage and shoulder blades through flaccid skin and dressed only in a loincloth fashioned from sacking staggered to a halt in front of them.

"Got anything to eat?" he whispered hoarsely. His eyes were merely deep black holes against the pale greyness of his emaciated face. Yellow pus oozed from an open sore on his stomach. "I'll tell you something if you got a bite."

Forrest regarded the man woodenly and his voice was as hard as his expression. "What you think, Rog? Reckon this one'll stew up good when he croaks?"

The man drew back in horror.

"Nah," Bell answered. "He ain't nothing but bone. Why don't they die with some meat on 'em."

"Olsen's looking for you, mister," the starving prisoner whined. "There, I told you. I reckon that's worth something."

"Sure," Forrest allowed, pushing past the man. "I'll send flowers to the funeral."

"You bastard!" the man snarled and spat, not having the strength to reach his target.

"How'd they ever get to call this a civil war?" Bell asked with a grin. "There just ain't no gentlemen left."

In the shelter, the smell of which no longer offended its new occupants as they grew to live with it, Hedges was again listening to the ramblings of the voluble West Point. The man had been one of the first prisoners into the rebel prison camp and was the sole survivor of the group of infantrymen captured at Antietam Creek. Alternately in the depths of depression or riding the crest of a happiness wave in a world of his own—dependent upon Olsen's willingness to accept further markers in exchange for heroin—he had only two topics of conversation. These comprised his only memories which revolved around cadet days at the West Point Military Academy—and his plan to act dead and be carried out of the stockade aboard the morning dead wagon. It was the latter subject which held Hedges' interest.

"It's the only way, Captain," West Point was saying as Forrest and Bell crawled in through the hole, their eyes distending against the darkness which came to the shelter each night since the bowl of the lamp had been burned dry of kerosene. "Guys have stormed the wall, tried climbing it at night and even dug tunnels. But it never works. You gotta go out through the north or the south gate. Then you stay in the dead house till it's dark and sneak away."

Forrest made a sound of disgust as he settled down in a corner, resting his back against the tin wall. "He's told everybody in the camp about that," the sergeant said sourly. "Maybe once it could have been done. But you can bet a million some sawbones runs a check on the bodies."

131

Hedges' eyes, as hungry as every other man's, stared through the meager light into Forrest's pale, unshaven face. "You come up with any better idea, Sergeant?" he asked softly.

"Ain't none," West Point put in.

"I ain't nuts," Forrest snarled.

"You've got no mind to blow," Hedges told him.

Forrest sprang into a crouch, his expression animalistic as he glared at the captain, leaning close to where Hedges was lounging. "No man's got any rank in here," Forrest rasped. "I could wipe you out and no questions asked."

West Point grinned idiotically from one man to the other. "Sic the bastard, Captain," he yelled.

The smile that crossed Forrest's face was as cold as it was insolent. "You gonna try to pull rank?"

Torture and malnutrition had slowed Hedges' reflexes, but he was still able to draw the razor with a speed of action that rooted Forrest to the spot. The point of the blade hovered a half-inch in front of the sergeant's right eye.

"Rank, no," Hedges said evenly. "This is something else."

The tension was thick in the malodorous hut and the silence it seemed to demand was almost painful against the men's eardrums. Nobody breathed for several seconds, until Forrest realized he had lost the argument. He rocked backwards, off his heels and sat down hard. He turned to look at Bell.

"First I nurse the crumb and then I give him back the only blade in the whole damn stockade. What do I get for it?"

Bell swallowed hard and didn't answer, his gaze fastened upon Hedges.

"Maybe a ticket to the outside," the Captain said softly.

Forrest was about to snarl an acid reply, but then

he detected something in the quiet tones and placid expression of Hedges which pierced his anger. "You want to tell it?"

Hedges showed his teeth and began to pare a thumbnail with the razor. "Fix him," he said, with an almost imperceptible nod in the direction of the happy West Point.

"For good?" Forrest asked.

"He don't deserve that."

"Hey, West Point," Forrest said and as the man turned towards him, lashed out with a fist. The knuckles smacked hard into the jaw and West Point fell over backwards with a sigh.

Hedges began to talk in soft tones as Forrest and Bell leaned close, listening earnestly to the plan. Outside the shelter the rotund, well-dressed Olsen also listened, then backed away and dismissed the four men he had brought with him. They moved away with reluctance, disappointed that there would be no head to crack tonight. But they obeyed Olsen's command because they knew that disobedience would mean a curtailment of the essentials and luxuries which enabled them to stay strong and healthy while their fellow prisoners wasted away around them.

As soon as the four had gone from sight, Olsen moved quietly back to the side of the shelter and crouched low, ear pressed close to the tin wall to catch the details of Hedges' escape scheme. He was still in the same position when Seward, Douglas, Scott and Rhett returned from a raid on the south side of the Sweetwater. It was Douglas who saw the eavesdropper and silently drew the attention of the others towards the crouching figure. He took Rhett around one side of the shelter as Seward and Scott moved stealthily in the other direction.

Olsen gasped in surprise as he heard a crunch of boot against dirt and looked up at Seward. Then he screamed and shot forward, powered by a vicious kick into the back of his crotch from Douglas. He yelled again as Seward bent a leg and cracked a kneecap against the fat man's jaw. Olsen pitched full-length and lay still.

"Your serve," Douglas said.

Seward shook his head as he looked at the unconscious man. "Looks like he don't want to play no more."

"What's the racket?" Forrest demanded, poking his head out through the hole.

Scott stooped, grabbed Olsen by the scruff of his neck and dragged him to the front of the shelter for Forrest to see. "You got company, Frank. Awful interested in what was going on inside."

"Olsen?"

Scott nodded.

"Toss him in the swamp," Forrest said vindictively.

"Bring him inside," Hedges countermanded.

The men on the outside looked at Forrest expectantly, aware of his change of heart towards Hedges over recent weeks.

"Do like the Captain says," Forrest said and glowered at the troopers, his expression warning them of the consequences of sarcasm.

Inside the shelter, Forrest and Seward held Olsen in a sitting position as Hedges slapped the man fore- and backhanded across the cheeks, jerking him to consciousness. His eyes snapped open, were dazed for a moment, then flooded with fear as he surveyed the ring of faces.

"Keep the lamp," he said quickly. "I'll get you some oil. No charge. I wouldn't take no markers from you gents."

Hedges smiled and showed him the razor. Olsen drew back as far as his captors would allow: but not out of range of the blade. Hedges reached out, grasped one of Olsen's hands and made a thin, shallow cut across the soft, flabby back of it. Olsen stared in horror at the trail of blood.

"My marker's better than any you've collected, fatso," Hedges hissed. "That's just a sample. No obligation. You don't want any more, just tell me what you heard."

Olsen forced his hand to his mouth and sucked off the blood. "All of it," he said suddenly as the faces pressed in closer around him. "I'd like to buy a place."

"How much you got?" Hedges asked.

"I ain't got nothing," Olsen rapped out. "My cousin down at the railroad depot's got all the markers. Close to a half million bucksworth. Soon as the war's over, we'll collect."

"You can't collect from dead men," Forrest put in as Olsen's round mouth sucked up more blood.

"Relatives maybe," Olsen answered quickly. "No guarantee in every case, of course. That's why I have to charge so high. Men die in here and maybe there's no relatives on the outside. I have to allow for those kind of losses. Any split you want for a place. Cut out my cousin if you like. He's a no-good bastard anyway."

"Runs in the family," Hedges said and slashed with the razor.

Olsen made a wet sound as blood bubbled in his gaping throat. As Forrest and Seward released their hold on the limp form, Hedges wiped the razor on the dead man's suit jacket.

"What's happening?" Rhett asked fearfully.

"We needed a body," Forrest answered, and turned a grin towards the New Englander. "If it hadn't been him, it might have been you."

"Jesus!" Rhett murmured.

"No good," Hedges put in. "Can't rely on him to stay dead."

It was apparent that no one expected the trial to last long. The hanging, if such there was to be, had been set for noon and it was after eleven when Railston prodded a shotgun into Edge's back to force him into the sunlit courtroom. It was not a large room, but every available square foot of public area had been packed with extra seating for those of the city's populace who needed to see that justice was done.

Lydia Eden sat tight-lipped and erect at the prosecutor's table, beside a grey-haired man who was big built but seemed somehow shrunken by the aura of self-righteous determination surrounding the woman. The twelve-man jury looked to be drawn from both farming and city stock and each of them glanced towards the small, black-clad woman for moral support as Edge ran his killer's stare over their faces. Her slight nod seemed to give them some comfort, but none would dare to meet Edge's gaze again.

The two court officers who had shackled Edge's hands behind his back in the cell while Railston held the shotgun levelled, took up positions at each side of the prisoner as Railston shoved him hard into a chair behind the defence table.

"Fine day for dying, ain't it?" the marshal muttered close to Edge's ear.

Edge looked towards the row of windows at one side of the courtroom and narrowed his eyes against the harsh glare of sunlight they admitted. Two of them were open and a fresh ocean breeze swirled in. As the babble of conversation from the public section died down, Edge could hear the surf hitting the beach.

"Rather wait until it snows," he said into the hush that had fallen over the room.

"Silence for Judge Ira Ryan," one of the court officers yelled and everyone in the court rose as a door opened behind a rostrum and a dapper, hawk-faced man shuffled through. The silence held until the judge had seated himself behind a fixed desk on the rostrum and cast an all-seeing, squint-eyed glance across the many faces before him. "Court's in session. You may be seated," the officer intoned.

Apart from the door through which Ryan had emerged, there were only two other entrances to the room. Both remained firmly closed. Edge settled back into his chair, convinced Paxton had either failed, or not tried, to find Emmeline Greer. But although his attitude was one of relaxation, his flinty eyes roved the room continuously, taking in its every detail. As the judge instructed the jury in a rich, Irish brogue and then launched into an oration on the prisoner's rights, Edge reached a decision. Crashing one of the windows was too dangerous and he had no idea where two of the doors led. The door which led to the marshal's office and cells was slightly ajar and offered an exit through familiar territory.

"Call Marshal Railston," the prosecutor opened as soon as the judge had finished his address.

Edge's expression was impassive as he listened to Railston's evidence of finding only one gun that had been fired in the back room of the Royal Flush saloon—Edge's gun.

"You represented, son?" Ryan asked when the prosecuting counsel had sat down.

Edge decided the judge was old enough to be his father and he liked the man's paternal manner. He wondered if Ryan's blandness would disappear when he passed sentence.

"Didn't want to take any debts to my grave, judge," Edge said evenly.

Ryan's expression darkened. "Smart talk won't get you anywhere," he snapped. "You want to question the marshal?"

"We ain't on speaking terms," Edge answered.

137

Laughter exploded from the public section and Ryan's eyes blazed with rage as he slapped his gavel on the desk. "I'll hold you in contempt!" he roared.

"I'll take that instead of the murder rap."

More merriment burst from the spectators and wasted several seconds before the banging of the gavel could quieten it. Blood vessels stood out from Ryan's brow as his rage reached a peak. He glared at Edge. "I'm withdrawing your right to speak again during this trial. If you utter another sound I'll have you removed to the cells and try you in your absence."

Edge knew the judge was not making an idle threat and emitted a low sigh as Ryan turned to the spectators and warned them of ejection should they interrupt the proceedings.

The coroner was called and, after he had received a nod of encouragement from Lydia Eden, told how both Shelby and Chadwick Eden had been killed with .45 caliber bullets. Abel Heffner had been seated at the rear of the public section and he pushed himself to the front with his head bowed when he was called to the witness stand. He mumbled the oath and then sat sideways to avoid a chance clash of eyes with Edge. The judge ordered him to face the court and the prosecutor asked him to tell his story in his own words.

"He shot Drew Shelby and Chadwick Eden," Heffner said suddenly, the words tumbling over each other as he looked everywhere except at Edge. "He come into the Royal Flush and we was having a friendly game of five-card draw—penny-ante stuff, you know? Then he comes in and starts upping the stakes. We're all winning so we go along. Then he starts to win. Lydia Eden's boy, he sees him cheating and calls him. He pulls a gun and blasts the kid. Drew Shelby went for his iron, but the cardsharp was already holding and he blasted Drew."

Edge glanced around the courtroom, unperturbed by the obvious effect the eye-witness account was having upon everybody present. His hooded eyes hovered momentarily upon each door, but none opened to admit Paxton and the woman.

"He's a damn liar, judge!" a shrill voice shouted from the public section.

As Lydia Eden and the marshal swung around to glare angrily towards the source of the interruption, Ryan made forceful use of his gavel to curtail the sudden burst of excited conversation.

"Who said that?" the judge demanded, squinting through the sunlight.

Edge allowed a low sigh to escape his pursed lips and turned his head slowly. Emmeline Greer, older and less desirable than he remembered, was rising to her feet at the rear of the courtroom. Beside her was Deputy Paxton. Both seemed to be in urgent need of sleep, but as they met the withering stares of Lydia Eden and the marshal, fear came to the surface, harder and far more positive than fatigue.

Edge looked back at the judge and saw him in concentrated study of Mrs. Eden and Railston a moment before glancing at the prisoner. The quizzical expression in his wise eyes invited comment.

"Think my case has arrived, judge," Edge said quietly into the expectant silence that was clamped over the courtroom.

"You want to call a witness in your defence, son?" the old man asked.

Edge nodded. "Maybe two."

Ryan looked at the confused Heffner. "Get off the stand," he instructed.

"Objection!" the prosecuting counsel yelled as Lydia Eden dug him hard in the ribs with a bony elbow.

"What grounds?" Ryan snapped, crooking a finger

139

to beckon Emmeline Greer and Paxton to the floor of the court.

The lawyer's red face became lined with a frown of thought. "Defence didn't inform the state of intention to call witnesses," he blurted out.

"You ask defence?" Ryan posed.

The prosecutor swallowed hard and sat down suddenly. Beside him the woman rested clenched fists on the table and stared straight ahead, her eyes glassy. The men of the jury began to whisper to each other, unsettled by this new turn of events.

"Silence!" Ryan roared at them, then looked back at Edge. "Which one you calling first?"

"Let's be polite," Edge said. "Emmeline Greer."

Ryan nodded and waved the whore onto the witness stand. As she took the oath, Paxton moved to stand beside Edge, carefully taking a wide circle around the taut bulk of Railston, who followed his progress with hate-filled eyes.

"Kept her holed up at my place last night," the young deputy whispered close to Edge's ear. "She was okay till we got to court."

"How'd you make her open up?"

"Stuck my Colt up her butt. Told her she could have two and a half grand in the bank or lead in her pants."

"Generous with my money," Edge muttered as the court officer took the Bible away from the woman.

"Proceed," Ryan said.

"Tell it like it was," Edge said evenly, his blue eyes meeting hers and locking on them. They looked at each other across the hushed silence and it was as if the woman was hypnotized by the power of the man's steady stare.

Her pale lips moved silently for a few moments before she found her voice. "Shelby and Heffner were cheating at cards," she said suddenly, continuing to

140

concentrate upon Edge, knowing that if once she clashed eyes with Lydia Eden or Railston, she would dry up. "They took Chadwick for a lot of money." She cleared her throat and seemed to gain confidence. "The stranger told Chad he'd been taken. Chad got angry and Shelby pulled a gun. He made to shoot Chad, but then turned it onto the stranger. The stranger saw it coming and drew. He plugged Shelby. Shelby's gun went off and the bullet hit the lamp. Then it hit Chad. The stranger fired in self-defence. Chad died because of an accident—a wild slug."

"She's a liar," Lydia Eden screamed, leaping to her feet. "She's a whore and a liar. She wasn't even there. Chad never consorted with whores."

Ryan gavelled the courtroom into silence. "Any reason the jury should believe your witness, son?" he asked Edge.

"You got anything else to say, Emmeline?" Edge asked the woman. "About how you came to be in the back room of the Royal Flush?"

She sucked the inside of her cheek and took time to reach a decision. "Okay, I'm a whore," she said suddenly. "But I'm not allowed to keep a quarter of what I make. I work in a plush place. We get rich clients. Shelby and Heffner paid me good to steer loaded suckers to their games."

Noise erupted again, but died instantly as Ryan raked his angry eyes across the excited and enraged faces. Heffner was seated at the front of the public section, staring down at his hands clasped in his lap. Attention was divided between him and the woman on the witness stand.

"What about after the shooting?" Edge asked.

Her teeth found her lower lip now and her eyes showed a more specific fear. But there was no menace in Edge's expression. "I got scared," she said.

"Of who? Heffner? Me?"

She shook her head. "Mrs. Eden. Scared of what she'd do if she found out I'd steered her son to the Royal Flush. I slugged you with a bottle, scooped up as much money as I could and got out of there. I figured to stay undercover until things had blown over. But Mrs. Eden sent a buggy for me. A couple of strong-arm guys hustled me into it and took me to the Garden of Eden. They said I had to stay there until the trial was over. But Vic Paxton came to get me. That's it."

"Any questions?" Ryan demanded of the prosecuting lawyer.

The man looked at Lydia Eden, but the old woman seemed to be in a trance, her hooded eyes held in an unwavering stare ahead of her.

"No questions," the counsellor replied.

"Go say your piece, Deputy," Edge said to Paxton.

There were no interruptions now as the spectators waited anxiously for new excitements. Paxton was sworn in and at a nod from Edge, gave his evidence, telling how Railston had taken two guns from the Royal Flush, of the dented lamp suggesting a ricochet and of finding Emmeline Greer under guard in the Garden of Eden.

"Somebody's got to die!" Lydia Eden screamed, her voice shrill and vibrant in the silence which followed Paxton's final words. Her hand came up and she pointed an accusing finger to where Emmeline Greer stood, pressed against the wall beside the defence table. "The harlot. If she took my little boy there, she is responsible for his death. She must hang."

The prosecutor reached out a hand to try to restrain the woman, but she knocked it away with a violent sweep of her arm.

"This court don't work that way, Mrs. Eden," Ryan said.

"Someone has to die!" the old woman screamed. "Chadwick must be avenged!"

Railston had backed away from the front of the court and was standing in the aisle which divided the public section into two. He was sweating freely and a nervous tic was sending spasms of movement across his left cheek.

"Getting too hot for you, Red?" Edge said suddenly.

"No witness leaves this court till I say so!" Ryan snapped.

Railston wasn't the fastest man in San Francisco, but his two gun draw was adequate for the occasion.

"You'll never make it," Edge hissed at the court officers as their hands moved to holstered revolvers.

"I've got the drop, Judge," Railston snarled, backing up the aisle.

The spectators looked on in shocked silence, none wishing to get involved in a fight they had no part of. Ryan showed no fear as he turned his eyes towards the jury, commanding their attention by sheer power of character.

"You boys want to retire to consider your verdict?" he asked easily.

The twelve men sought tacit advice from Lydia Eden, but the old woman was still venting silent hatred upon Emmeline Greer, completely detached for her surroundings. The foreman cleared his throat. "Don't rightly know," he said, and flicked frightened eyes towards the back of the court, where Railston had reached the door.

"Well, I'll tell you, boys," Ryan said slowly. "Way I see it, certain people have conspired to pervert the course of true justice here today." His head moved, and his cold eyes hovered momentarily upon a succession of individuals before him. "Namely, a rich woman full of spite; a cardsharp, a coroner and a marshal. Now I reckon those others did it for a piece

143

of the rich woman's fortune. They committed perjury for gain is how I see it. And whether you stay in here or go out to talk it over, there better be only one verdict. If it's the wrong one, I won't be able to think anything else but that you been bought, too."

"Objection!" the prosecutor barked.

"Shut your damn mouth," Ryan told him as the jurymen put their heads together. Ryan allowed them less than half a minute. "Well?"

The foreman blinked. "We say he's innocent, Judge," he said hoarsely.

"Set the prisoner free," Ryan said as Railston backheeled the door, crashing it wide.

But nobody moved, held in frozen attitudes by the menace of Railston's guns. The tic in the marshal's cheek began to work more frantically as a hundred pairs of eyes fastened upon him.

"Wasn't such a good day after all," Edge rasped across the stillness.

"Somebody has to die!" Lydia Eden screamed.

Paxton's gun exploded and wood splinters flew from the front of the witness stand as he fired through it. The bullet thudded into the wall above the doorway and showered plaster on to the marshal. As women screamed, Railston spun on his heels and vanished from the doorway. Those closest to the door waited until the sound of his footsteps had diminished and leapt forward, staring after the retreating figure.

Ryan got to his feet and snapped orders at Paxton, demanding the arrest of Lydia Eden and her conspirators. The old woman began to scream for vengeance and could not be silenced until one of the court officers clamped a hand over her mouth. The second man unlocked Edge's handcuffs.

"Obliged," he said, rubbing the red marks left by the circles of metal. When he stood up and looked

144

towards the windows he could see the gallows in a shaft of sunlight at the center of the yard beside the courthouse. Somewhere across the city a clock began to strike noon. He turned his eyes towards where Emmeline Greer was still pressed against the wall, looking exhausted by the strain and fear she had experienced. He stepped in front of her. "I ought to kill you," he said softly.

She put a hand to her throat. "You told the deputy I could keep the money."

He showed his teeth in a cold grin. "You saying you took a bribe to give evidence?"

She looked away from him, to where Paxton and the court officers were shepherding their prisoners through to the jailhouse under the steely-eyed gaze of the judge. "I hid it in my room," she told him softly.

Paxton halted beside them, looking at each in turn. "You sure don't look like a man just saved from the gallows," he said.

"I'm happy inside," Edge told him without emotion. "Obliged for your help."

"If Railston hadn't cracked, it could have gone the other way."

The remainder of the spectators had filed out of the courtroom, disappointed that the excitement was over and there was to be no hanging as a climax.

Edge grinned. "Only the good die young. I figure I'm immortal. You going after Railston?"

Paxton's mouth tightened. "The judge said to arrest him."

Edge nodded. "You got as long as it takes me to collect my bankroll and find him."

The young deputy toughened his expression, but his tiredness still showed through. "I'm the law now. It's my job."

Edge took hold of the woman's arm and steered her towards the door which led to the jailhouse. "Guess we all got to do our own thing," he muttered. "I need my guns."

Paxton followed him into the marshal's office and gave him his gunbelt with the Colt in the holster, and his Winchester. From a cell, Lydia Eden stared with seemingly sightless eyes at Emmeline Greer. Heffner and the coroner were in the cell vacated by Edge. Mint Julep was sleeping off the effects of the wine Paxton had given him.

"I did you a big favor," Paxton said to Edge. "Return it. Leave Railston to me."

Edge regarded him coldly. "I said I was obliged."

"That's all your life's worth?"

"Some would say less than that," Edge replied, hustling Emmeline Greer out into the hot California sun, breathing deeply of the free air.

CHAPTER NINE

The morning dawned damp and misty and in the grey light the dead wagon seemed more funereal than usual as it rolled in through the north gate. Forrest and Seward heard it before they saw it, straining their eyes towards the sound of creaking harness and springs, the squeak of an ungreased axle. Twice men shouted and the wagon halted. There was the sound of the driver and his companion jumping down and then low-voiced conversation punctuated by the thud of a body heaved over the tailgate.

The dead wagon always entered the stockade unescorted, manned by two Confederate soldiers who were not armed. By tacit agreement, it had immunity to harrassment, for the prisoners did not relish the sight of decomposing bodies littering the camp and co-operated in their removal.

"We got us a stiff," Forrest called as the wagon rolled out of the mist, bringing with it the sickly odor of the many bodies which had ridden in it.

"Don't sound so goddam happy about it," Hedges hissed from within the shelter.

The driver and the man beside him on the box seat had faces to match their job, the sallow flesh drooping in melancholy arcs under their eyes and around their mouths. Even the two-horse team looked sad.

"Where is he?" the driver asked, dropping to the ground with a sigh.

"Inside," Seward said, jerking his head towards the shelter.

"Regulations state you got to bring him out," the second man said.

Forrest shook his head. "He don't smell good. We're not touching him."

Seward glanced around. Visibility was down to about a hundred feet and nothing moved in front of the encircling curtain of mist. It was just as they had expected, for unless prisoners had a cadaver to be rid of, they stayed well clear of the dead wagon, many believing it emanated ill-luck, others fearful that it was disease ridden.

"We could leave him," the driver said to his partner. "Let the maggots start on him. Couple of days maybe he'll crawl out on his own." He laughed harshly.

"Worth half a pound of tobacco if you go in and get him," Forrest offered.

Both the driver and his partner took on expressions of greed. "You buy it off Olsen?" the second man asked.

"He got his cut," Forrest confirmed.

"It's a deal," the driver said. "Come on, Chuck."

He stooped and went in through the hole, his partner close behind him. Hedges was stripped to his underwear but the driver didn't see him, for his attention was upon the sprawled body of Olsen. When he did realize something was wrong, it was too late. Hedges grasped him around the neck and tightened his long fingers, forcing his thumbs hard against the man's windpipe. The man's eyes grew wide and he tried to struggle, but Douglas, who was also without his top clothes, sank a fist hard into the heaving stomach, knocking the fight out of the driver. The second man had time to emit a gasp of surprise before Scott silenced him with an edge of the hand chop to the back of his neck. As the man pitched forward, Bell let go a mighty kick, the toe of his boot smashing into the face and throwing back the head with a sharp crack of breaking bone. Hedges released his grip on the driver and the stale air trapped in the dead man's lungs hissed out as his limp form sank to the dirt floor.

"Okay out there?" Hedges called in a hushed whisper as Rhett and Scott began to strip the rebels of their uniforms.

"Sun won't be long showing, sir," Forrest answered quickly. "Mist won't stay long."

"We're not going to make it," Rhett said in trembling tones as he jerked the driver's pants down.

"At least you're getting your fun," Douglas said, shrugging into a grey tunic.

"Cut out the gab," Hedges ordered, pulling on the driver's pants, snatching a glance at West Point, still deep in the arms of a drugged sleep.

"It's clearing already," Seward said urgently. "Hurry it up, for Christ sake."

Hedges finished buttoning the tight-fitting tunic,

hoisted West Point and struggled with him out through the hole in the wall. The mist had not retreated, but its color was noticeably brightening by the moment. Beyond the walls of the stockade a bugle sounded.

"Get it in the wagon," he ordered, moving to the rear and tossing West Point over the tailboard without ceremony.

Forrest and Seward took a final glance around and hoisted themselves up and into the back, looking with distaste at the crumpled forms of the two dead bodies sprawled there.

"Move it," Hedges snapped into the shelter and hauled himself up on to the box seat of the wagon as Rhett, Bell and Scott crawled out and ran to the back, scrambling aboard. Douglas brought up the rear, still buttoning his tunic and Hedges had set the team moving so that the bogus rebel had to throw himself up at the seat.

Hedges brought the team around in a tight turn and checked a desire to slap them into a gallop towards the gate at the end of the street.

"I feel like a duck in a shooting gallery," Douglas said out of the corner of his mouth as he peered ahead, trying to pierce the thinning greyness of the mist.

"You can get off any time you like," Hedges told him.

All around them, the camp was waking up, the prisoners moving out of their stinking shebangs to relieve themselves and contemplate a new day of misery that could not be eased so conveniently.

"I guess a sitting duck's got a chance," Douglas answered.

"Better than these guys," Hedges agreed, watching the prisoners scurry away from the dead wagon.

"You weren't long," a guard called from a sentry shack atop the wall at the side of the gate.

149

Both Hedges and Douglas kept their heads down as the gate was swung open by the fumbling Mint Julep. "Dying ain't what it used to be," the captain drawled in reply as he clucked the horses forward, through the gateway.

"How many you got?" Mint Julep called as the wagon rolled by him.

"Two we're sure of and six that could be playing possum," Hedges answered.

Douglas gasped and Hedges grinned at him as the drunken guard giggled with glee. "Don't get nervous, Douglas," Hedges said through pursed lips. "Crew of the dead wagon always crack one with him. It gives old Mint Julep a kick."

In the rear of the wagon, Forrest risked a glance over the tailgate and an involuntary grin spread across his pared face as he saw the gate slammed closed. Another bugle split the air. The mist seemed to hear it as retreat and began to lift. On the seat of the wagon Hedges and Douglas looked to their left, between the cookhouse and the bakery, across the swamp to where the dead house took on solid shape in the clearing air of the new day. Ahead, the track that was Main Street grew longer, curving towards the railroad depot at the center of Anderson. On each side of the street were the camps of Confederate soldiers, each dominated by a fort.

"I itch all over, Captain," Douglas said. "We must be surrounded by at least two thousand Johnnie Rebs. And it feels like every one of them bastards is pointing a carbine at me."

But the soldiers treated the dead wagon with the same degree of repugnance as the prisoners and stayed well clear of it. Ahead of the wagon, a track spurred off to the left, leading across the swamp and bridging the Sweetwater towards South Street and the route to the dead house. Hedges was aware of the geography because many of the roads surrounding the stockade had been built with prison labor and West Point had done his share of the work.

"Just keep thinking that way and you won't do anything stupid," Hedges said softly as he held the team on a straight course along Main Street towards the village, passing the spur.

The leading curve of the sun had breasted the horizon now and strong shafts of yellow warmth were dispelling the remnants of the mist. The many tiny noises of mass humanity coming out of sleep and going about their morning chores formed a discordant concerto of sound, but to the men aboard the wagon its creaking progress was like a continuous thunder roll, masking everything else. And the sun felt like a blazing spotlight, pouring scorn upon their escape attempt.

"Can't we hurry it up a little, Cap?" Forrest hissed from inside the wagon.

"Getting nervous?" Hedges answered without turning his head.

"I don't hear you doing no singing," the sergeant shot back.

"Takes a worried man," Hedges said. "I ain't that anxious yet."

They had reached the edge of the village and the sound of the wagon's progress was magnified as it rolled along the deserted street between the blank faced façades of buildings. But the train whistle, although distant, was shrill enough to reach every strained ear of the escapers.

"Christ, we're early," Rhett exclaimed.

"Better than being late," Seward told him on a note of rising confidence as the wagon wheels rattled over the tracks and Hedges steered the team into a right turn, halting it within the depot.

An aging man in South Western livery looked at

the wagon with disinterest. It had never been brought into the village before, so he failed to recognize it for what it was. The fact that it was army warned him not to ask questions. The approaching train, rattling down from the north section of the track, whistled again and the note of the locomotive altered as the engineer eased back on the throttle. It hissed into the depot, dragging a line of ten passenger cars.

"Anderson! Andersonville Prison! Only military personnel alight here."

The conductor's voice was shrill above the snort and hiss of the locomotive, which had halted several yards short of where the wagon was parked. Hedges clucked, and slapped the reins, urging the team forward until the seat was level with the footplate. The fireman grinned cheerily at Hedges and Douglas as car doors opened on the far side of the train.

"Nice morning," he said brightly.

"Short one," Hedges answered, bringing his hand away from the back of his neck and thrusting it towards the smiling man.

The point of the razor entered the man's throat just above his Adam's apple and went in to the hilt. He died soundlessly, with his mouth wide, bubbling foamy blood. On the other side of the footplate the engineer was leaning out, looking down the side of the cars. Hedges stepped across to the locomotive and lowered the fireman's body as Douglas opened the front flap of the wagon.

"All aboard," he muttered to those inside, and followed Hedges.

A bell clanged and the conductor shouted. The engineer turned around and froze his expression, waxen in shock. He saw the slumped body of his crewman, the menacing attitude of Hedges with the razor extended, and the cold grins of the men crowding off the wagon and on to the locomotive.

"Ain't you got a schedule to keep?" Hedges asked softly as the conductor shouted again.

The engineer began to tremble. Hedges moved up to him, spun him and held the razor hard against the crotch of his coveralls.

"Ain't cold," Hedges whispered close to his ear. "But there's more than one way to castrate a monkey."

"Please," the engineer rasped, reaching for the controls. "Anything you say."

His nervous hands sent too much power to the drive and the wheels spun on the rails. He fed sand to them and eased his grip on the throttle. Metal found traction on metal and the locomotive inched forward. Hedges watched every move the engineer made, noting the response he received from the straining locomotive. Around him he could sense the slackening of tension from the men as the train snaked out of the depot and the speed built up.

"Why'd you have to kill my partner?" the engineer asked in shaking tones as the prison buildings and the surrounding military installations slid away behind the speeding train.

"We know how to stoke the fire," Hedges answered, and looked towards the men.

They began to feed logs into the glowing firebox.

"I think we're hauling too much weight," Forrest yelled.

Hedges leaned from the cab and peered back along the track. The village looked peaceful in the morning sun and in the last few seconds before it disappeared behind an intervening stand of pines, the dead wagon was still undisturbed. But the South Western Railroad man was walking towards it.

"So get rid of the excess," Hedges told Forrest.

As the Captain continued to peer over the engineer's shoulder, Forrest hefted a sledgehammer from two brackets and climbed up on to the tender.

"Nobody knows how to drive?" the engineer asked suddenly.

"Somebody's learning," Hedges told him as the sound of furious hammering rose from behind the tender.

Swaying precariously between the straining locomotive and the first passenger car, Forrest swung the hammer at the coupling pin. As it came free, the locomotive surged forward, leaving the cars to roll to a halt when their momentum was expended. Forrest climbed back across the tender. As he dropped on to the footplate he put a boot under the dead fireman and tipped him over the edge.

"He was just dead weight, too," he said to Hedges with a grin.

"Mister, there's more to driving a train than pulling handles," the engineer whined suddenly.

"Where's West Point?" Bell yelled.

"Jesus," Rhett answered.

"I didn't bring him." This from Scott.

Hedges glared at Forrest.

The sergeant shrugged. "He was no use for nothing, Captain. He didn't do nothing 'cept gab and sleep."

The Captain's hooded eyes moved over each haggard, unshaven face and saw in every one an expectation of his anger. "So how was he different from you?" he hissed.

"Pressure's falling!" the engineer croaked.

The men, at a command from Forrest, hurried to feed logs into the firebox.

"What about it?" the engineer wanted to know.

Hedges withdrew the razor, wiped the blade on the man's denims and slid it back into the pouch. "You're more use than some I know," he said, turning to look out over the country speeding by. "That buys you a ticket to ride."

"Captain?" Rhett called after a half-minute of silence among the men.

"Yeah?"

"I reckon the Union Army is west and north of here, sir. We're heading south. How we going to get back?"

They were steaming through country which reminded Hedges of Iowa. There was cotton on the fields instead of wheat and the plantation houses were more ornate and less functional than the farm buildings of the Middle West. But, now that the horrors of Andersonville were left behind, Georgia looked tranquil and untouched by the ravages of war.

He sighed. "We'll get back," he said, too softly for the men to hear. "How, is another story."

❉   ❉   ❉

It took Edge all afternoon to track down the marshal after he had retrieved his money from Emmeline Greer. Information was not hard to come by for the word had been spread that Red Railston was no longer a power behind a badge and there were many who had suffered under his dictatorial rule.

The trail led north from the city, along the oceanside boundary of the Garden of Eden. At first Edge followed horse tracks in the sand, but Railston was a big man and he pushed his mount too hard. He had left the animal to die from exhaustion in the surf. Edge ended its terrified pain with a bullet from the Winchester before heeling his own horse forward, following the heavy imprints of the man's boots.

The endless sky above the infinite ocean was becoming tinged with pink when he saw his quarry, hobbling in useless haste far ahead. He demanded only a steady canter from his horse and asked for no more speed even when Railston heard his pursuer, twisted his head for a look back and broke into an ungainly run. To one side the ocean barred escape while the solid height of a cliff face was an insurmountable barrier in the other direction. Railston could only go forward and he kept going until his legs finally folded beneath him and he pitched into the sand.

Edge, his burnished face an impenetrable mask of hardness, rode a few more yards and dismounted. Railston turned his head and Edge could see the grains of yellow sand clinging to his sweat-run face.

"If you stay down, you won't have to fall when I kill you," Edge called to him across the regular pounding of the surf.

He had halted, some ten yards short of where Railston lay. He stood with his legs apart, body twisted in a half turn to present a narrower target to the marshal.

"You got turned loose," Railston said breathlessly. "Let it be."

Edge released the reins of his horse and the animal moved up the beach, searching for grass. "You railroaded me, Railston. You slugged me and put me behind bars. You shouldn't have done that, feller." His right hand closed over the butt of the holstered Colt.

Railston licked his lips and spat out sand. He got unsteadily to his feet. His hat was tugged by the wind off the sea and he reached up to hold it in place. Edge snatched out his gun and fired. Railston looked at the blood spouting from his hand, then down at the sand where his severed thumb lay. The pain reached him and he screamed. "Christ, you didn't even give me a chance!"

"No better one than you gave me," Edge told him and squeezed the trigger again. The bullet drilled a hole through the wrist of Railston's good hand.

"Hold it!" A voice cut across the pounding surf.

Railston was helpless and Edge risked a glance over his shoulder. Paxton was riding towards him at a gallop. When Edge returned his attention to Railston, he saw that the man had taken several backward steps. Blood from his wounded hands dripped down to form patterns in the wet sand at the tideline. Railston moved again and water rushed in around his boots, splashing up his legs to leave dark patches on the pants of his high-priced suit.

"You won't shoot me with Paxton around," the marshal said, his face twisted by pain but his voice ringing with confidence.

Behind the man the sky turned from pink to deep red as the sun made contact with the horizon.

"You want to bet on it?" Edge asked, aiming the Colt.

Railston took two further backward steps and made a pathetic attempt to reach for his guns. But his useless hands merely brushed the carved butts.

"You lose," Edge muttered and shot the man in the center of the forehead. His dead weight fell backwards and made a great splash that sprayed Edge with salt water.

Paxton side-slid his horse to a halt and sprang from the saddle.

"I told you to hold it!" he yelled at Edge in high-pitched anger.

Edge didn't turn to look at him. "He went for his gun."

He watched the body of the dead man get tossed by the broiling surf, lost it for a few moments, then saw it again, floating easily on the gentle swell further out. Then a current of the outgoing tide took a grip on Railston and sent him, floating like a fat log, towards the vast crimson pool where the sun dipped into the ocean.

Paxton's tone became flat and devoid of fury. "He's so full of meanness, he should have sunk like a stone."

Edge shook his head as he turned to look for his horse. "Come morning, maybe. Right now Red sails in the sunset."

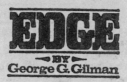

EDGE

►BY◄
George G. Gilman

Josiah Hedges is no ordinary man — he's a violent gunslinger. Created out of fury, hardened by death and destruction, he's rough, but not as rough as the fate of those who get in his way.

Over 3.5 million copies sold!

☐	40-504-9	Loner	#1	$1.50
☐	40-505-7	Ten Grand	#2	1.50
☐	40-506-5	Apache Death	#3	1.50
☐	40-484-0	Killer's Breed	#4	1.50
☐	40-507-3	Blood On Silver	#5	1.50
☐	220668-8	Red River	#6	1.25
☐	40-461-1	California Kill	#7	1.50
☐	220750-4	Hell's Seven	#8	1.25
☐	220704-1	Bloody Summer	#9	1.25
☐	40-430-1	Black Vengeance	#10	1.50
☐	220600-1	Sioux Uprising	#11	1.25
☐	220669-6	Death's Bounty	#12	1.25
☐	40-462-X	Hated	#13	1.50
☐	220624-1	Tiger's Gold	#14	1.25
☐	40-407-7	Paradise Loses	#15	1.50
☐	40-431-X	Final Shot	#16	1.50
☐	220795-9	Vengeance Valley	#17	1.25
☐	220856-9	Ten Tombstones	#18	1.25
☐	220894-0	Ashes and Dust	#19	1.25
☐	220948-4	Sullivan's Law	#20	1.25
☐	40-008-9	Rhapsody in Red	#21	1.25
☐	40-487-5	Slaughter Road	#22	1.50
☐	40-485-9	Echoes of War	#23	1.50
☐	40-486-7	Slaughterday	#24	1.50
☐	40-488-3	Violence Trail	#25	1.50
☐	40-202-3	Savage Dawn	#26	1.25